AMBUSHED!

Hank stared, unable to comprehend what was happening. He saw the slugs smash into Thomas's body, saw the bright red stains flowering on the white shirt. Thomas was thrown backward by the shots, his legs hitting the sideboards of the wagon. He tumbled out and landed heavily on the gound.

"Grandpa!"

The scream tore out of Hank's throat, and while it still echoed in the clearing, he grabbed for one of the Henrys in the wagon. As his fingers closed on the stock, he saw out of the corner of his eye the other mounted man drawing his gun. The draw was smooth and fast, and Hank knew that his own stunned effort was too slow. He ducked as the man fired, dragging the rifle along with him.

The bullet smacked close by his ear. Hank hit the ground and rolled, levering a shell into the rifle's chamber as he did.

EPITAPH

L.J. WASHBURN

POCKET BOOKS

New York   London   Toronto   Sydney   Tokyo   Singapore

POCKET BOOKS, a division of Simon & Schuster Inc.
1230 Avenue of the Americas, New York, NY 10020

Copyright © 1987 by L. J. Washburn
Cover art copyright © 1990 Peter Caras

Published by arrangement with M. Evans & Company, Inc.
Library of Congress Catalog Card Number: 87-32770

ISBN: 0-671-67187-1

First Pocket Books printing July 1990

10 9 8 7 6 5 4 3 2 1

POCKET and colophon are registered trademarks of
Simon & Schuster Inc.

Printed in the U.S.A.

For James M. Reasoner,
Shayna Leigh,
and Joanna Lynn

EPITAPH

One

*I*t was going to be another hot day, Hank Littleton thought as he stepped out the front door of his grandfather's house. Not even nine o'clock in the morning and already the sun was beating down with a fierce, brassy intensity. There was something about Texas in the summer that made a man sweat just thinking about it.

The sound of hammering diminished as Hank walked along the dirt road. Thomas Littleton was working at his chosen profession in the big, cluttered backyard behind the house.

He was making a coffin.

It was a big burden to put on a man's shoulders, asking him to be the county sheriff as well as the local undertaker. Thomas hadn't felt like he could refuse, though, when folks asked him to take on the job. His son, Enos, Hank's father, had held the job for several years, and now that he was gone, Thomas was the only man in town with any law enforcement experience.

Hank was on his way to check for messages at the sheriff's office in case anyone was looking for his grandfather. He had to pass by the Cougar Saloon, and he noticed that there were several horses tied to the hitchrail even this early. The place did a good business, being one of only two saloons in San Saba. Its owner, Mose Duncan, believed in stopping trouble before it started, and it was seldom that Thomas was called to the Cougar to stop a fight.

Hank heard raucous laughter from inside as he passed the batwings. Glancing into the gloomy interior of the saloon, he saw three men leaning against the bar and tossing back shots of whiskey. He didn't recognize any of them. They were tall, lean, and wore dusty range clothes. They also all wore pistols in low-slung, tied-down holsters.

Hank knew if there was any trouble that Mose had a sawed-off shotgun underneath the bar, and he was a pretty fair hand with a bung-starter, too.

Hank moved on past the saloon and hurried his pace a bit as he saw a strange wagon coming down the street toward the sheriff's office. Two men Hank had never seen before were seated on the wagon.

He had just unlocked the door of the office when the sudden blast of a gunshot behind him made him spin around.

The flat crack of a six-gun was followed by the dull boom of a shotgun. Hank saw one of the strangers from the saloon come staggering through the batwings, clutching a bloody arm. More shots followed from inside the saloon.

Hank jerked open the office door and ran inside. There was a rack on the wall holding several Henry rifles. He snatched one of the rifles, grabbed a box of cartridges from a drawer in the desk, and began to load the Henry on the run as he raced back outside.

His grandfather would probably raise hell with him for getting involved in this, he thought. But he was the closest one to the trouble, and he *was* a deputy, sort of. Out of the corner of his eye, he saw that the man driving the wagon had reined in his team and pulled a gun from his holster. The man was looking intently down the street, ready to fire if need be.

Hank ran toward the saloon. A sudden howl of pain came from inside the building. What few pedestrians were on the street were now scattering, looking for cover.

The man who had run out was mounted on his horse now and was galloping down the road away from the place. The shooting had stopped abruptly, leaving an ominous quiet. Hank was twenty yards away when the other two men burst out, guns in hand. One of them spotted Hank and twisted around, bringing his pistol up. Hank dove for the dirt.

He landed heavily, knocking the breath out of himself as the man's gun blasted. Hank heard the whine of a bullet passing by close overhead. He was in an awkward position, but he squeezed the trigger of the Henry anyway. The butt of the rifle kicked back painfully against him. The shot didn't hit anything, but it came close enough to make the men leap for their horses. They dug in their spurs and the animals spurted away from the hitchrail.

One of the men turned and snapped off two more shots in Hank's direction, making him hunker lower to the ground. Then the gunman spurred after his partner, who was already several yards ahead of him.

Mose Duncan staggered out through the batwings of the saloon, a bright red stain on the side of his shirt. "They robbed me!" he yelled in a strangled voice. "Somebody stop them!"

Hank rose to his knees, jacked another shell into the chamber of the Henry, and lifted it to his shoulder. The first holdup man, who must have been wounded by Mose's shotgun, was out of sight now, and the other two were rapidly fleeing. They were at least seventy-five yards down the street already. It was going to be some tough shooting.

Hank took a deep breath and settled the sights of the rifle on the back of one of the men. He hesitated just a second, then slowly squeezed the trigger just as his father had taught him.

The Henry boomed and belched fire and smoke. The holdup man threw up his arms and flew out of the saddle.

Enos Littleton had been a good teacher when it came to shooting, if nothing else. Hank had to admit that much.

As he shifted the sights over to the other holdup man, Mose Duncan let out a groan and fell into the street, raising a cloud of dust that obscured Hank's vision for a moment. Hank waited for the dust to clear, then fired again. His target jerked and swayed but stayed in the saddle.

He didn't fall off until the horse had covered at least another ten yards.

Hank stood up slowly and stared down the street, blinking. The motionless shapes of the two men didn't seem like anything human as he looked at them. They looked more like dolls that had been thrown away carelessly by some kid.

People were starting to poke their heads out of their hidey-holes to see if it was safe to come out. A couple of storekeepers walked tentatively into the street to make sure the two robbers were dead.

A voice behind Hank exclaimed, "Good Lord, man, that was some shooting! I've never seen anything like that."

Hank looked around to see that the second man had climbed down from the wagon. The stranger wore a wool suit that had to be stifling in this heat and a bowler hat. He had a diamond stickpin in his cravat and a carefully waxed handlebar mustache that was growing more limp with each passing second.

Hank looked past the fancy-dressed man to the one still sitting on the wagon seat. He might have been a cowhand, judging from his run-over boots, worn clothing, and battered old Stetson. But there was a hardness in his ice-blue eyes as he slipped his gun back in its holster. He regarded Hank with something like appreciation.

Breathing deeply and wishing that his heart would quit beating so fast, Hank said, "I generally hit what I aim at." That was true enough, but until this morning, he had never aimed at anything except targets and wild game. There was something very different about shooting at a man, especially one who was shooting back at you.

"Whooo-eee!"

Hank looked over at the sidewalk and saw a young boy standing there, his face glowing with excitement. Jimmy Maxwell had always looked up to Hank like a big brother, and Hank didn't mind having him around as long as he didn't make too big a pest of himself. Jimmy could get underfoot without really meaning to, though, and he was reckless.

"You should've headed for cover when the shooting started, Jimmy," Hank told him as he walked over to the sidewalk, letting the muzzle of the rifle droop toward the ground.

"And miss seein' my pal Hank shoot down them owl-hoots? No, sir!"

Hank gave a tired grin, trying to cover up the twinge he felt inside at the reminder he had just killed two men. He turned to the man in the bowler hat and asked, "Could I help you, mister?"

The stranger looked up at him, seeing a tall young man with thick blond hair and broad shoulders that stretched the simple cotton shirt he wore. "I was looking for Sheriff Thomas Littleton," the man in the bowler hat said, "but I was expecting an older man. . . ."

"Hank ain't the sheriff, mister," Jimmy piped up. "Shoot, he ain't but fifteen years old."

The man in the bowler hat looked surprised as Hank shot a glare at Jimmy. He was used to being taken for older than he was, but there was no need for Jimmy to go making an issue of his age. Out here on the frontier, a fifteen-year-old was considered a man most of the time. And back east, there were a lot of *men* not much older than Hank who were wearing Confederate gray or Union blue in this year of our Lord 1863. Wearing those uniforms—and dying in them. Anyway, he was nearly sixteen.

"The sheriff's my grandpa," Hank told the stranger. He glanced down the street and saw an older man hurrying toward them, a Colt in one hand and a Winchester in the other. "Here he comes now."

Thomas Littleton strode up, his lined face taut with tension. He was almost as tall and brawny as Hank, and his white hair was still thick. "What happened here?" he asked. "Are you all right, Hank?"

"I'm fine, Grandpa. Somebody better tend to Mose, though. He's been shot."

Thomas glanced over Hank's shoulder and saw several townspeople hovering around the recumbent saloon-keeper. "I'm sure somebody's already sent for Doc Yantis. Anyway, Doc always comes to check on any gunplay. You haven't answered my question, boy. What happened?"

The man in the bowler hat stepped forward. "Sheriff, my name is Reuben Reed, and I can tell you what happened. Your grandson there just stopped a holdup and killed two would-be robbers."

Thomas looked intently at Hank and saw that he was pale under his tan. "Is that true, Hank?" he asked softly.

"Yes, sir," Hank nodded. "There were three strangers in the Cougar. I guess they tried to steal Mose's money. I heard him cut loose with that scattergun of his, and then the other fellas started shooting. I . . . I shot those two when they tried to get away."

"What about the third one?"

"He got away, but he was wounded. Looked like Mose got him."

Thomas sighed heavily. Violence was uncommon in San Saba, but it always saddened him when it did occur. He and Mose Duncan were friends, had been for a long time. "I'd better see how Mose is doing. You sure you're all right?"

"I'm fine, Grandpa." Hank's voice was stronger, and some of his color was returning.

As Thomas started to turn away, Reuben Reed caught at his arm and said, "Excuse me, Sheriff. I wonder if I could discuss some business with you."

"After I've seen to my friend's welfare," Thomas replied stiffly. He went down the street toward the cluster of figures around Mose Duncan.

Jimmy Maxwell said, "Maybe now your grandpa will give you a deputy's badge to wear, Hank. You think so?"

"I don't know, Jimmy." Hank took a deep breath again. The reaction he had felt immediately following the shooting was beginning to wear off. He knew, though, that nothing would ever really be the same again. Not now. Not after he had killed.

He could see the sun shining on old Doc Yantis's bald head as he worked over Mose Duncan. Doc stood up, snapping his bag shut, and ordered several of the bystanders to take the saloonkeeper down the street to his office.

"How's Mr. Duncan, Grandpa?" Hank asked when Thomas had rejoined them.

"Doc says he should be all right. The bullet missed anything important and just tore up some muscle. If Doc can stop the bleeding, Mose should make it."

Hank nodded gratefully. He liked Mose Duncan.

Reuben Reed was still standing nearby, fidgeting impatiently. He started to step forward and speak to Thomas again, but before he could do so, Thomas put a hand on Hank's arm and said, "Let's go in the office and talk."

Hank swallowed. He had a feeling Thomas was going to do most of the talking.

Reed said, "Sheriff, I do have some business to discuss with you."

"I'll be with you in a minute, mister. You can wait out here if you like or find you some shade, but I'll get to you when I can."

Reed frowned but didn't say anything. Thomas and Hank went through the door, and Jimmy started to trail along behind. Thomas held out a hand to stop him. "You run along home, boy," he said, firmly but not too harshly. "I want to talk to Hank by himself."

"Well, okay," Jimmy said grudgingly. "See you later, Hank." He went down the street, pretending to shoot at imaginary badmen.

Thomas shut the door and went to his paper-cluttered desk, sinking wearily into the chair behind it. He put the rifle and pistol he carried on top of the welter of papers. Hank replaced the Henry on the wall rack, then waited to see what his grandfather had to say.

"What in the blue blazes did you think you were doing?" Thomas suddenly asked. "You could've gotten killed trading shots with those men!"

"They held up the Cougar Saloon," Hank replied. "I figured it was my job to stop them, me being the closest one and all."

"Catching robbers is my job, not yours. You ain't an official deputy, and you know it." Thomas sounded angry, but his tone abruptly softened as he went on, "Dammit, boy, I don't want to see you hurt. What would your pa say if I let you get killed fighting outlaws?"

Hank stiffened at the mention of Enos. "You think he'd really care?" he asked.

Thomas stared down at the desktop for a long moment, not sure what to say. "You see things in a mighty harsh light, Hank," he finally said. "They're not always what they seem like."

Hank was silent. He held himself tightly, waiting for his grandfather to finish.

"Well, hell," Thomas sighed. He let a grin steal over his face. "You're old enough to know when you're taking a chance. And once you took a hand, you did a damn good job. That must have been some shooting."

Hank relaxed slightly. "I was probably lucky."

Thomas shook his head. "I've seen you shoot. Luck don't have that much to do with it." He stood up, coming around the desk to put a hand on Hank's shoulder. "Sure makes you stop and think, doesn't it?"

Both of them knew what he was talking about.

In a voice that was little more than a whisper, Hank said, "When it was happening, all I was thinking about was stopping them and keeping them from hurting anybody else."

"I know. I wish I could tell you it gets easier, but it doesn't. There are times out here when a man has to fight to defend himself or other people. You get backed into a corner, and there's only one way out. But every time you have to kill, it hurts you, too. Remember that, Hank." Thomas's hand tightened on his shoulder in reassurance. "Maybe you won't ever have to face that feeling again."

Hank returned his grandfather's smile and felt better. Thomas wasn't one to talk a lot, but what he said usually made sense.

"Guess I'd better see what that stuffed shirt outside wants," Thomas went on, going to the door and opening it. Reuben Reed was leaning against the wagon, mopping his forehead with a handkerchief. He looked up as Thomas said, "All right, Mr. Reed, I've got a lot of work to do, so state your business."

"Of course," Reed replied, tucking the handkerchief back into his pocket. "I understand you're the local undertaker."

"I am."

Reed's expression became solemn as he said, "Sir, I wish to hire your services. I need you to build a coffin."

"All right. Sorry to hear about your loss."

Reed shook his head. "No, sir, you don't understand. This is a rather special coffin. If my associate and I could talk with you privately . . . ?" Reed looked nervously up and down the street.

With a frown of puzzlement, Thomas said, "Go on in the office. I'll be back as soon as I tend to something."

The bodies of the two robbers were still sprawled in

the street. Thomas called several men over and told them to take the corpses down to his house. When the men had started on their errand, Thomas stepped back into the office and saw that the other man from the wagon had joined Reed.

Glancing at Hank, Reed frowned slightly and said, "I believe it would be best if we talked alone, Sheriff."

"Hank's my grandson," Thomas said. "I don't keep secrets from him."

"I understand, sir, but the need for secrecy is great. I must insist."

Thomas started to tell Reed he wasn't in a position to insist on anything, but he bit back the words. He was curious about this bowler-hatted, out-of-place individual, and he didn't much like the looks of the other one. It might be better to find out what they were up to.

"Hank, you head on down to the house," Thomas said, holding up a hand to forestall the protest he knew his grandson would make. "I told some of the boys to take those owlhoots down there, and you best see that they did like I told 'em. I'd appreciate it, son."

"All right," Hank said with a grudging nod. "I'll see you later, Grandpa."

He went back out into the hot sunlight, surprised that Thomas had asked him to leave. He had expected his grandfather to tell Reed to get on with what he had to say or get out. It didn't really matter that much, though; Hank figured he could get Thomas to tell him about it later.

Jimmy Maxwell was waiting down the street for him. Hank put a smile on his face. The boy was probably going to talk about the shoot-out for days, so he supposed he had better get used to it.

Two

Thomas sat down behind the desk again and motioned for Reed to take the chair opposite. Reed took off his bowler hat and balanced it on his knees as he sat. The other man leaned against the wall next to the door.

"Now what's all this about, mister?" Thomas asked.

"Well, as I said, my name is Reuben Reed. This is my associate, Gus Ordway."

Thomas nodded to Ordway, who returned a like greeting.

"We're here to see you about a coffin," Reed went on. "Not a regular coffin, mind you, but a specially constructed one with some rather, ah, unusual features."

Thomas felt an instinctive distrust of this man, and he didn't much like Ordway's looks, either. "What's unusual about a coffin?" he growled. "Long as it's built good and tight, what more do you need?"

Reed took a piece of paper from an inside pocket. "I have a diagram here of what we need—"

"Reuben." Ordway spoke for the first time, his voice cold and stony. "Maybe you'd better be sure Sheriff

Littleton is interested in taking the job before you show him that."

"Yes, yes, of course." Reed nodded nervously. *"Are* you interested, Sheriff?" He watched Thomas intently.

"I'm curious," Thomas said after a moment's pause. "You still haven't told me who's dead."

"Why . . . no one, Sheriff. No one at all."

Thomas's shaggy eyebrows drew down in a startled frown. "What do you mean nobody's dead? Why the hell else do you need a coffin, if not to bury someone in?"

"I see that I should show you my credentials," Reed said tentatively. He reached into his pocket again and withdrew another folded sheet. He extended it across the desk to Thomas, who took it and unfolded it.

Thomas's frown deepened as he saw the official seal and scrawled signature underneath the note requesting assistance. "Jefferson Davis," he breathed. "You telling me that the President of the Confederacy sent you boys all the way to San Saba?"

"Not to San Saba specifically, no," Reed admitted with a slight smile. "But we are on a special mission for President Davis, and you can be a great deal of help to us."

Thomas studied the paper. He wouldn't know Davis's signature from George Washington's, but the seal looked authentic enough. The paper was heavy and expensive, the kind a president would use. Finally, he nodded and handed the paper back to Reed. "All right. Tell me about it."

Reed replaced the letter in his jacket and leaned forward again. "As you no doubt know, sir," he began in conspiratorial tones, "the Confederacy has many friends and allies in Europe and other places. Our forces are in need of weapons and supplies that could come from any number of sources . . . if not for the damned Yankee blockade."

Thomas nodded. He had heard about the blockade along the East Coast and knew that the South was starting to feel the pinch of it. But what that had to do with him, he couldn't see.

"The War for Southern Independence has been going rather badly of late for that very reason," Reed went on. "We must have another route for supplies to enter."

Thomas began to see the light. "You want to bring guns in through Texas," he said.

Reed and Ordway both looked grim as Reed went on, "We have an arrangement with a man in Juárez. He can provide the weapons that the South needs to win the war and throw off the shackles of the North, sir. But he insists on payment in full . . . and he insists on being paid in gold."

"You're carrying the gold with you?"

Ordway answered, "Half a million dollars' worth."

Thomas leaned back in his chair, trying not to stare. This talk had taken a crazy turn. Here he was, in the familiar old sheriff's office with its fraying wanted posters tacked on the walls and the battered coffeepot sitting on the stove, and these strangers were talking about more money than this whole county had ever seen.

"A man shouldn't haul around that much gold," he said slowly. "Lots of folks'd like to get their hands on it."

"We know that all too well, Sheriff," Reed said. "That's why we've come to you."

Thomas shook his head emphatically. "I don't want the job of guarding it, no, sir."

"That's not what we want. You see, there are Yankee agents swarming all over the state. They know that President Davis sent men here to buy guns. They'd like nothing better than to discover our identities and steal that gold from us. The Confederacy can't afford that, sir," Reed said solemnly. "We're appealing to you to help us."

Thomas took a deep breath and tried to grasp what he had been told. He *was* a southerner, he supposed; his parents had come to Texas from Mississippi. But out here on the frontier, a man forgot things like that. He was a Texan, born and raised, before he was a Confederate.

But he was also a law officer, duty bound to help other representatives of the government, even if the seat of it was way the hell off in Virginia.

"What do you need me to do?" he asked.

"We need a coffin with a false bottom," Reed said, indicating on the diagram how the box was to be made. "We can carry the gold in the hidden compartment. The Yankees won't suspect something like that. We'll just be two men taking their dear departed father home to be buried."

"Thought you said nobody was dead."

"I don't think anyone will insist that we open up the coffin," Reed said.

Thomas thought a moment longer, then said, "It won't work. Not in Texas in the summer. You bury a man where he dies; you don't take him anywhere else unless it's somewhere you could reach in less than a day."

"Then that will be our story. We'll simply say that we're going to some community close by."

Thomas shook his head. "Still seems risky to me."

"Less risky than carrying the gold under a sheet of canvas in the back of a wagon," Ordway put in. "That's what we've been doing."

Thomas's eyes widened in alarm. "You ain't got it in that wagon outside right now, have you?" he asked.

"No, we cached it outside of town where we made camp," Reed explained. "We have a few other people traveling with us, not enough to draw attention but sufficient to serve as guards. They're watching over the gold."

"You're mighty trusting of them, seems like."

Reed smiled. "They are as devoted to the cause as we are ourselves, I assure you."

Thomas picked up the diagram of the coffin and studied it with a professional eye, noting the details of its construction. It could be built the way they had it, he decided, but already he saw some ways of doing it better.

"Reckon you know what you're doing." He laid the paper on the desk, tapping it with a blunt finger. "I can build it for you. I will build it for you. When do you need it?"

Reed heaved a sigh of relief. There was a flash of triumph in Ordway's hard eyes. "As soon as possible," Reed said. "Can you bring it out to our camp when it's ready?"

"I suppose I can. Where is this camp?"

"A few miles east of here, near where the San Saba River runs into the Colorado."

Thomas nodded. "I can find it."

"How long do you think it will take?"

Thomas glanced at the diagram again, doing some quick figuring in his head. "Ought to be done tomorrow. I can probably bring it out to you late in the afternoon."

"That would be fine," Reed said eagerly. "Are you sure you can have it ready by then?"

"I won't work on anything else until I'm done with it. Course, I can't promise that something won't come up that I have to tend to as sheriff. I've got my duties here."

"Certainly, certainly. We understand that." Reed chuckled. "That grandson of yours is really something. I never saw the like, the way he went after those robbers."

"Hank shouldn't have done that," Thomas said stiffly. "He could have gotten himself hurt."

"Well, he's a fine shot, that's for sure. You must be very proud of him. You can see why I didn't want to discuss our business with him around, though. It was for his own good, really. The less he knows about this matter, the less interest any Yankee agents might take in him."

Thomas didn't think that was the real reason Reed had wanted Hank out of the office. The man was just full of himself and his secret mission, enjoying the drama of the situation.

"Now, there's just the matter of your fee to be settled," Reed went on, drawing a wallet from his pocket.

Thomas held up a hand to stop him. "You can pay me when I deliver the goods. And all I want is ten dollars."

Reed looked baffled. "But the job is worth much more than that to us," he protested. He glanced at Ordway, who shook his head sharply, evidently understanding the reason behind Thomas's words.

"That'll cover the materials," Thomas said. "You've asked me to help out my country. I won't put a price on that."

"You won't take anything for your labor?"

Thomas shook his head.

"Very well." Reed replaced the wallet in his pocket. He stood up and held out his hand. "I'm glad you're helping us, Sheriff. I can't tell you how important this is."

Thomas shook the man's hand, finding his grip rather flaccid, as expected. Ordway didn't offer to shake hands.

"I'll get busy on it," Thomas said. He watched the two men leave the office, and a moment later heard the creak of wheels as the wagon pulled away.

Not even noon yet, and already more surprises had happened today than usually occurred in a month in San Saba. From the violence of the holdup to the arrival of the two Confederate agents with their story of gold and guns, this had been a very unusual morning. Thomas hoped it wasn't the start of something. He liked his life peaceful.

There were still the bodies of the two robbers to be attended to. Like he had told Reed and Ordway, there were some things you couldn't put off, not in this heat. Thomas folded the diagram of the special coffin and stuck it in his pocket. He had everything on hand that he would need for it, and he would get started as soon as the two holdup men were safely in the ground.

He left the office and headed toward his home.

* * *

Hank was glad when the job of burying the two robbers was done. Corpses had never bothered him much, since he had been raised in Thomas's house and had known about his grandfather's business as far back as he could remember. To him, death was a natural part of life.

Until today. Today was the first time he had been responsible for those bodies that he and Thomas had put in the ground.

It was the middle of the afternoon before they finished that grim chore. The robbers had had a little money in their pockets, but not enough to pay for the plain coffins Thomas had used for them.

Hank drove Thomas's wagon back around behind the house. His grandfather sat on the seat beside him, quiet and lost in thought. As Hank unhitched the team and put them back in the barn, Thomas sat on the ground in the shade of one of the big pecan trees. He took a piece of paper out of his pocket and studied it.

Hank wondered if the paper had anything to do with the business Thomas had discussed with the two strangers this morning. So far nothing more had been said about it, but Hank couldn't help but wonder.

Thomas motioned for Hank to come over and held the paper out to him. "Take a look at that and see what you think," he grunted.

Hank studied the drawing for a moment, then said, "Looks like it wouldn't be too much trouble to build, but why would anybody want to?"

Thomas took a deep breath. "Those fellers didn't want you knowing about this, Hank, but I don't see any reason not to tell you. I guess they're just naturally suspicious, being in their line of work, but I know you can be trusted."

"Sure, Grandpa." Hank's curiosity was really up now.

Quickly, Thomas outlined what he had been told by Reed and Ordway. Hank nodded and frowned, not understanding the situation exactly at first, but it came clear for him as Thomas explained. "You can see why they wanted the whole thing kept a secret," Thomas finished.

"I reckon. Seems kind of strange to think there might be Yankee agents around this neck of the woods."

"Seems that way to me, too, but I suppose it's possible. We really don't know a lot about the war, or the way it's being fought. Those two seemed sincere enough."

Hank trusted his grandfather's judgment, and he was glad Thomas had decided to take him into his confidence. "I won't tell anybody about this, not any of it," he assured his grandfather.

"Especially not that pesky Jimmy."

Hank laughed. "Especially not Jimmy." His face became more serious as he went on, "I guess you'll be needing my help with this job."

"I will if I'm going to get it finished tomorrow."

Hank nodded and didn't say anything. He had been very quiet during the burial of the two outlaws, too.

"Are you all right, son?" Thomas asked after a moment. "I know it's hard, all that's happened today."

"I'm fine," Hank said. "I've been thinking a lot, but I guess that's not so bad."

"No. It's not." Thomas extended a hand, and Hank helped him up. Thomas felt a surge of pride as he looked at his tall young grandson. It was sometimes hard to believe that Hank wasn't any older than he was. The boy had always been quiet and smart beyond his years.

Thomas guessed he hadn't done such a bad job with him.

Slumping on the ground with his back against the trunk of a tree, Hank watched the sun slide below the western horizon. It had been a long day, and he was tired. He had spent the rest of the afternoon working with his grandfather on the special coffin for the Confederate agents.

He hoped that Reed and Ordway appreciated the effort. He and Thomas had worked without stopping ever since their return from the cemetery. The job was half done;

they'd be able to finish it in the morning, and then take it out to the camp by the river in the afternoon.

Thomas was still hammering, driving a few last nails into place before calling it a day. The old man seemed tireless at times, dredging more strength out of his wiry body than seemed possible. Now he took the nails out of his mouth and dropped them into one of the pockets of his apron. He brought the hammer with him as he came over to the tree where Hank was sitting.

"I reckon I can still beat you when it comes to working, boy," Thomas said with a faint smile. "Don't know what's going to come of you young folks. You don't seem to have as much stick-to-itiveness as your elders."

Hank didn't know what to say to that, so he kept his mouth shut as his grandfather sank down onto the ground beside him. The two of them sat there in silence for a few moments, watching the sun set. A little breeze had sprung up from somewhere, giving scant but welcome relief from the heat. As shadows began to fold around the backyard, the stirring of the wind actually seemed cool.

"You think we'll be finished with the coffin in time, Grandpa?" Hank asked, leaning his head against the tree and closing his eyes.

"Should be."

Hank hesitated, then said, "I sure never expected the day to turn out like this when I woke up this morning."

"Neither did I. Most of the time, though, important things come up on you sudden like." Thomas smiled. "I reckon if we knew they were coming, we'd worry too much about 'em."

That made sense to Hank. He pushed himself to his feet and said, "I guess I'll go rustle some supper."

"No, I'll do that." Thomas got up slowly, his muscles having stiffened while he was sitting. "You go on down to town and make sure nobody's been looking for me."

Hank frowned. Thomas had sent him to the sheriff's office this morning on the same errand, and he had wound up trading shots with outlaws. "You sure you want me to?"

"I'm sure," Thomas nodded. "Get on with you."

Hank went, slipping his hands into the pockets of his pants. There was a ball of nervousness in his stomach as he walked down the street. He didn't think anything else unexpected was going to happen today, but he hadn't expected the attempted robbery, either.

He could accept the part he had played in the day's events. He hadn't wanted to kill the two men, but circumstances had left him no choice. He wasn't blaming himself.

But ever since he had come to that realization, another question had been plaguing him: if it ever happened again, how would he react? Would he let his instincts take over, as they had this morning, or would he stop to think about it and maybe wind up dead himself?

Thomas watched Hank disappear into the gathering dusk and knew what the boy was feeling. The old saw about getting right back on the horse that had throwed you had a lot of truth in it. A person couldn't give in to worry about what might happen, or that's all he would ever have time for.

Lamps were visible through the windows of the houses Hank passed. There were still a few riders and wagons on Main Street, but most of the day's traffic was over. As he went past the Cougar Saloon, he saw that the doors were closed and locked. He wondered how Mose Duncan was doing. The Red Top, across the street and farther down, was doing a good business. Everybody was sorry that Mose had gotten shot, but that wouldn't stop them from patronizing the competition as long as the Cougar was shut down.

There was movement in the shadows along the sidewalk up ahead. Hank about halfway expected Jimmy Maxwell to pop out, eager to talk about the robbery and shoot-out.

Instead, the figure that appeared was taller than Jimmy, and Hank heard the swish of a dress.

"Hello, Hank," a female voice said. He stopped in his tracks. Rose Ellen Hobbs came toward him on the sidewalk, smiling shyly. She stopped a couple of feet away and laced her fingers together. She didn't look up at him, but she seemed to be waiting for something.

"Hello, Rose Ellen," Hank made himself say. That ball of nervousness in his stomach had just swelled up some more. Rose Ellen was a nice enough girl, but damned if she didn't make him uncomfortable. Every time she was around she seemed to expect him to say or do *something,* only he wasn't sure what.

"I heard about what happened this morning. You must be a real hero."

Hank didn't see how shooting a couple of holdup men made him a hero, but Rose Ellen sure seemed impressed by it. He didn't know if he liked that or not. Rose Ellen wasn't as big a pest as Jimmy, but she could make him feel pretty funny. She was a year younger than he was, and right pretty, he supposed. Her long blond hair seemed to glow with a light of its own, even now in the dusk. It was really nice when the sun shone on it. . . .

When he didn't say anything, she went on. "I think you were magnificent, saving Mr. Duncan's life like that."

"You heard how Mose is doing?" he asked, finally finding his tongue again.

"My pa said he was going to be all right. At least that's what Doc Yantis was saying down at the general store earlier."

"I hope so. I like Mose."

Rose Ellen cast her eyes down again. "I've never met him. Mama says proper ladies don't associate with saloon men and they certainly don't go into such places. Have you ever been in a saloon, Hank?"

"Sure. Lots of times." It was no boast. He had been

in both the Cougar and the Red Top with his grandfather, but Thomas wouldn't ever let him take a drink.

"I don't see why ladies can't go into saloons. Mama said she wasn't surprised Mr. Duncan got himself shot, what with the kind of low-lifes who hang around saloons."

"The men who robbed the Cougar weren't from around here," Hank said, feeling compelled for some reason to defend the establishment. "Leastways, I never saw 'em before."

"I'm sure they were desperate men. Why, if I had seen them shooting at you, I would have fainted dead away."

"Reckon it all happened too fast for that." Hank wished he could think of some way to graciously get past Rose Ellen and go on to the sheriff's office. He could see the building down the street, though, and it didn't look like anyone was waiting there.

"It must have been really exciting. . . ." Rose Ellen's voice trailed off wistfully. Not much out of the ordinary ever happened in San Saba; today's attempted robbery was the most excitement in months, all right.

And Hank was starting to wish he hadn't had any part in it.

Suddenly, Rose Ellen stepped closer to him. He frowned and started to say, "What—" She put her hands out, rested them on his arms, and lifted her face to his. Before he knew what was happening, her lips were pressed to his. They were warm and wet and didn't taste anything like what he would have thought. Somehow his arms wound up around her, hugging her up against him, and that feeling was sort of unexpected, too.

She took her mouth away from his and whispered, "I know you must think I'm terribly bold, Hank, but I just had to know what it feels like to kiss a hero!" She slipped out of his embrace and started to hurry down the sidewalk. "I've got to get home. Pa's going to kill me if I miss supper."

Hank's heart was pounding like it had after the gunfight, and his mouth was dry again. He watched Rose Ellen hurry away, then suddenly realized that she hadn't said what it was like to kiss a hero. Maybe she had been disappointed in him. Hell, he'd done more shooting in his life than kissing!

He grinned sheepishly and shook his head. For a second there, he had shared her opinion that he was a hero, and Hank knew good and well that wasn't the case.

He was just a young fella in a little Texas town. No, sir, he wasn't a hero.

Thomas Littleton sat on his front porch in a rocking chair that his father had brought from Mississippi. Thomas's grandfather had made the chair, back before the turn of the century. There was something comforting about its age. Thomas wasn't the sort of man to get sentimental about a piece of furniture, but he did like that chair.

His pipe glowed in the shadows. All the lamps in the house were dark now, and Hank was asleep in his room. Thomas liked to come out here at times like this, to savor the peace and quiet and reflect on the events of the day. He rocked slowly, the slight creak of the chair blending in with the night noises of insects. There was still a breeze, thank goodness. The night was turning off downright pleasant.

A shape loomed up in the shadows of the yard, a figure that resolved itself into a human form as it came closer. Thomas stayed where he was, not worrying. He knew who this nighttime visitor was.

"Hello, Thomas." The woman came up onto the porch.

"Evening, Dorene. Sit a spell."

"I believe I will." Dorene Pierson sat in another rocking chair beside the one which Thomas's grandfather had made. Thomas had built this one, and it was every bit as sturdy as the other. "How's Hank?" Dorene asked.

"Bearing up pretty well." Thomas sent a cloud of

smoke puffing up from the pipe. The breeze caught it, shredded it, made it blend in with the shadows. "It hit him hard to realize he had killed two men, but I think he understands he didn't have a choice once he got involved."

"You must be proud, him stopping a holdup like that."

"Part of me wishes he'd kept out of it . . . but I reckon you could say I'm proud of him."

"His daddy would be, too."

Thomas's tone hardened somewhat. "If he was here, I'm sure he would be."

"You can't blame Enos for wanting to help defend Texas, Thomas. With so many men off in that war, the Rangers are all we've got between us and all those outlaws and Indians."

"Maybe he's got a good reason for being gone now," Thomas said stubbornly. "That don't change all the times he's been gone since Hank was born. Hank doesn't hardly know his father, and the boy resents it. He don't say much, but I know it bothers him."

"I suppose it was just too hard for Enos to stay around much after Margaret died." Dorene sighed. "I never saw a man and a woman more in love than those two."

"He could have stayed for the boy's sake. . . ." Thomas's voice trailed off. Both of them were silent for long moments. Thomas turned his head to study the features of the woman in the dim light from the moon and stars.

He knew Dorene Pierson's face quite well. He was familiar with the quiet strength and dignity there. There had been a time when she was a beauty, but the years had changed that, taking away some of the superficial attractiveness but leaving the quality below. She was still a damned handsome woman, in Thomas's humble opinion. She moved with the grace of a young girl, and when she let her long dark hair down, it was a glorious wonder, thick and lustrous and only lightly touched with gray.

He loved her, he supposed. There wasn't any other way to explain it.

She had come to San Saba five years earlier to live with her married daughter after the death of the husband she had loved for twenty-five years. That beloved husband and that daughter had never known all the truth about Dorene. They had never known her the way she had been when Thomas first met her in New Orleans, more than thirty years gone now. To this day, Thomas couldn't help but smile when he thought about that French Quarter bawdy house—and Dorene.

Even with all the changes time had wrought, he had recognized her as soon as he saw her in San Saba, and she had known him. He had pretended not to know her as her daughter introduced the two of them, and he had seen the gratitude in her eyes. It was natural enough that they would become friends, since they were near the same age. Only they knew that the friendship had rekindled something much more.

She flatly refused to marry him, though, saying they were both too set in their ways. Thomas had to admit that she was probably right. There was nothing stopping them from enjoying each other's company, however.

"I can't see your face very well, Thomas, but I can tell you're thinking," Dorene said softly.

"Thinking about how pretty you are," Thomas answered, a slight gruffness trying unsuccessfully to conceal his feelings. "Thinking about how you looked the first time I saw you, there at the Countess's house."

"It's a good thing it's dark on this porch, Thomas Littleton," she said tartly. "Imagine, making a poor woman blush that way!"

"You blushed right nice back then, too."

"You hush." It was said quietly, caressingly.

Thomas enjoyed the gentle bantering, but he was having a hard time concentrating on it. His worry about Hank, the secret job he had been given by Reed and Ordway—those were things that kept a man's mind occupied. He wondered if he should tell Dorene about the special coffin, then decided against it. The Confederate agents probably wouldn't be too happy about him telling Hank. He had to have help, though, if he was going to finish the job as quickly as they wanted. They'd just have to be reasonable about Hank's knowing.

He had lapsed into silence again, and Dorene said, "My Lord, Thomas, you're the most preoccupied man I ever saw tonight."

"You told me to hush," he pointed out.

"Well, if you can't think of anything better to do than sit there and stare out at the night, I might as well go home."

"Stay," he said. He reached out and found her hand in the darkness. "Stay."

Three

The campfire was a necessary risk. There had been no Indian depredations in this area for quite a while, and the party camped by the San Saba River wasn't worried about being attacked by bandits. Any desperadoes who attacked this group would get more than they bargained for.

There were two wagons, the mules that pulled them, and a remuda of eight horses. One of the wagons was a covered Conestoga, the other was the vehicle Reuben Reed and Gus Ordway had taken into town. They were parked several yards apart, and the fire was built in between. Reed knelt beside the blaze, keeping an eye on the bacon and beans as they cooked. He and Ordway had brought back fresh supplies from town. The heat from the flames made sweat run down Reed's broad face.

A tall man strode toward the fire from one of the wagons. He wore a dark, subdued suit and a white linen shirt, and the only touch of color about him was the bright cravat knotted around his throat. His hair was gray and thinning, but his pleasant, unlined face belied his true age.

"Will our dinner be ready soon, Reuben?" he asked.

"Yes, sir, Mr. Clayborne."

Abner Clayborne sighed. "Dining on the prairie once more. How the mighty have fallen, Reuben."

"You make me sick, the way you poor-mouth all the time, Abner," a female voice said from behind Clayborne.

The tall man turned and saw a young woman in her early twenties standing there. She wore an expensive dark blue gown that was beginning to show the hardships of living on the trail. Her thick dark hair was parted in the middle and fell in waves to her shoulders, framing a beautiful but pale face. Her expressive green eyes flashed with anger at the moment, and her mouth was a tight line across her features.

Clayborne frowned at her and said gently, "Now, Louise, is that any way to talk? You certainly are jumpy."

Louise Shelby opened her mouth to respond sharply, then thought better of it. She restrained her fury with a visible effort.

"How about some coffee, Miss Shelby?" Reed asked, getting to his feet. He hoped that Clayborne and Louise weren't going to fight again. You could never tell what Clayborne would do when he got angry.

Clayborne moved behind Louise and reached up to lay his hands on her shoulders. The muscles there were rigid with tension. Clayborne's strong fingers dug in, rubbing and kneading, and Louise started to relax in spite of herself.

"Damn you, Abner," she said huskily. "Every time I get mad at you, you do something like this."

"I don't like seeing you upset, my dear."

She turned to face him, shrugging off his grip. "And I don't like you dwelling on the past. It's gone."

The words were spoken quietly, but they struck Abner Clayborne like a blow across the face. He stiffened, and his right hand clenched into a fist. His arm stayed at his side, though, and he didn't smash that fist into Louise's face, the way he felt like doing. That wouldn't bring Twin Oaks back, wouldn't bring back the life that had been taken so abruptly and so violently from him.

Another voice spoke up nearby. "Is anything wrong, Louise?" A younger woman came into the circle of light cast by the fire. She was little more than a girl, really, no more than seventeen, her figure slim and lithe. Her blond hair was pulled back and tied with a bow which made her look even younger.

"Nothing for you to worry about, Beth," Louise said, smiling at her sister.

Clayborne forced a smile and said to Beth Shelby, "That's right, we were just talking about old times. But there will be better times in the future, won't there?"

"I hope so," Beth said. "Things have been so difficult since we left Georgia."

"Well, those days are coming to an end, dear girl."

Reed stepped up to the little group with the cup of coffee for Louise in his hand. She took it from him and started back toward the wagon, saying, "Come along, Beth. It's time we started dressing for dinner." The sarcasm in her voice wasn't lost on Clayborne.

Clayborne and Reed watched the women disappear into the back of the wagon. Reed turned back to the meal he was preparing, while Clayborne stared off into the darkness.

Clayborne didn't really see anything except his memories of the plantation called Twin Oaks. The memories were bitter ones, recollections of slaves who ran away and soldiers who confiscated everything of value, of a once glorious estate falling into disrepair and ruin.

Abner Clayborne had always been a survivor, a man who came out on top. He was going to get there this time, as well.

Ignacio Jiménez came up to the fire from tending the remuda. He was muttering to himself in Spanish as he removed his battered sombrero and used his sleeve to wipe away sweat on his forehead. In the glow of the fire, the weathered skin of his face and hands looked like old saddle leather. The creased sockets of his weary eyes were deep-set. His hands were large, callused, and coarse-knuckled, but there were none gentler with horses.

"Supper's about ready, Jiménez," Reed said. "Go get Gus."

Jiménez walked slowly into the woods. Ordway and the final member of the group, Bob Smith, were out in the woods standing guard over the camp. Ordway would eat first, then Smith would take his turn.

There was movement in the darkness, and Bob Smith said, "That you, Jiménez?"

"Yeah. Reed says for Ordway to go on in and eat."

"I'll pass the word." Smith faded back into the shadows.

Jiménez shook his head. It was strange the way those two seemed so at home in the night. They were both dangerous men, with that lean look of a wolf. Jiménez knew you couldn't judge a man solely by his looks, though.

Jiménez had never known a more ruthless man than Abner Clayborne, and he looked like someone's friendly uncle.

He would be damn glad when they reached El Paso. Then he could take his share and slip over the border. He had relatives in Chihuahua who would be glad to see him—and the money he would have.

Inside the Conestoga, Louise Shelby brushed her hair with short, angry strokes while Beth sat on top of a trunk and watched her with a worried frown on her face. "I don't know why you and Abner have to fight so much," Beth said. "He's always seemed like such a nice man to me."

"He can be when he wants to," Louise replied. "He just gets so damned maudlin at times!"

Beth had gotten over being shocked at the language

her older sister sometimes used. She put it down to the fact that Louise had left home at an early age and had had a lot of men friends. Men talked that way, and Louise had picked it up. If she had stayed home, her parents would have never allowed her to curse, just as they had never allowed Beth to use words like *damn* and *hell*. Only preachers were allowed to say those words, and then only in sermons.

Beth wasn't at home anymore, though, and her parents were both gone, buried in the cemetery behind the little church they had attended. Since going to Atlanta to find Louise, Beth had discovered just how different the real world was from the vision she had had of it. Finding out that Louise was the mistress of a wealthy plantation owner who was much older was enough of a shock.

Once Louise had told her that she and Clayborne were leaving Georgia, Beth hadn't even considered not coming along. Louise was the only family she had left.

Louise could feel her sister watching her with those wide blue eyes. Beth was always watching her, always trailing after her like some overfriendly kitten. Louise put up with her, though. An older sister *had* to put up with a younger one. The girl was a total innocent, too. She wouldn't last a week on her own out in the world, not without winding up in a crib somewhere, using herself up to make money for some madam. Louise knew about that life.

And Abner Clayborne, for all his faults, had made it possible for her to leave that life behind. Now, if everything went well, they would all be rich.

Louise put her brush down and moved over to sit next to Beth on the big trunk. She slipped an arm around her and said, "I don't want you worrying about anything, darling. Everything is going to work out just fine, and we'll have a better life than we ever could have back in Georgia."

Beth nodded and tried to smile, then said a moment

later, "Louise, do you ever miss the farm? Do you miss Mama and Daddy? I . . . I do."

"Of course I do," Louise lied. "And I know you do, too. But don't you think that Mama and Daddy would want us to go on and make a good life for ourselves?"

Beth's smile became more confident as she nodded again.

"I'll bet you're hungry. You go get some supper from Reuben. I'll be along in a minute."

"All right." Beth hugged her sister for a moment, then went to the back of the wagon and hopped easily to the ground.

Louise stayed where she was, very aware of what was in the trunk on which she sat. Her long, slender fingers strayed down to the heavy lock that held the lid closed. There were only two keys that would open that lock. Abner Clayborne carried one of them, Reuben Reed the other. And either man would kill anyone who tried to take the keys.

She had seen the gold, and now her breath came a bit faster as she thought about the bars of metal that seemed to glint despite their dull color. They still had the letters CSA stamped into them, but that didn't matter.

They belonged to Abner Clayborne now, and that meant that eventually they would belong to her.

She patted the trunk with a proud smile on her face and then stood up. She was smiling when she left the wagon and rejoined the group gathered around the fire. Clayborne saw the expression on her face and came to her, slipping an arm around her waist and letting his hip rub against hers.

Louise didn't care. Let the old fool get lost in his memories of Twin Oaks. Someday he would be gone and she would still have the gold, and that would be enough.

Four

The sky was cloudy the next day, which cut down on the glare of the sun but did little else to relieve the heat. If anything, the damp, sticky air felt worse. Hank wiped sweat off his forehead, then reached down to get a grip on one side of the coffin.

"You ready?" Thomas asked from the other side.

Hank nodded.

"All right. Let's go."

They lifted, grunting under the weight of the big box. Hank was doing most of the lifting while Thomas was just balancing his side, but he didn't mind. He was young and strong and glad to help.

The end they were lifting thumped down in the back of the wagon bed. Hank and Thomas paused a moment to catch their breath, then went to the other end of the coffin. It only took a moment to raise it level and slide the box up into the wagon.

"I'm glad that's done," Thomas said. "Now all we've got to do is take it out there to their camp."

"Seems like a strange way to carry gold," Hank said.

33

Thomas snorted, "That much money usually brings nothing but trouble."

"Maybe so." Hank didn't sound overly convinced.

They had spent the morning and the early part of the afternoon finishing the coffin. The wood had been sanded and polished until it shone. The hardware was all new and gleaming. The inside was padded and lined with silk, all of which could be removed easily to get to the false bottom. Underneath that false bottom was the secret compartment, eight inches deep and running the whole length of the coffin. A lot of gold could be hidden there. When it was loaded, the coffin was going to be damned heavy, and Hank felt a little sorry for the team that was going to be pulling it. Just the coffin by itself weighed enough.

"You hitch the team up," Thomas said. "I'll be ready to go in a few minutes." He went into the house.

Hank paused long enough to get water from the pump, then went to the barn to get the mules. His stomach was rumbling; they hadn't taken the time to eat lunch, and evidently Thomas didn't intend to until after they had delivered the coffin.

Thomas emerged from the house as Hank finished hitching up the team. Hank was surprised to see that his grandfather had a shell belt strapped around his waist, and the old Remington revolver in the holster. Thomas also had a Henry rifle in each hand.

He tossed one of the rifles to Hank, who plucked it neatly out of the air. "What's this for?" Hank asked.

"I don't think we'll run into any trouble, but we won't take any chances. Better to be armed if some of those Yankee agents are skulking around. They might make a try for the gold while we're at the camp."

The weight of the weapon in his hands reminded Hank of what had happened the day before. He had slept better than he had expected to, having figured that the spirits of the two dead men would haunt his dreams, but despite his untroubled slumber, the memory of the violence was vivid. And he didn't want to get to the point where killing two men *wouldn't* bother him.

He climbed up on the wagon seat, holding the Henry carefully. Thomas joined him and picked up the reins, laying his rifle on the floorboards. It took several slaps of the lines to get the mules moving.

The air was heavy and unmoving, and Hank thought that there would probably be a storm later. "Think it's going to rain, Grandpa?"

Thomas shook his head. "I doubt it. Clouds like that just sit there and make you miserable and then finally break up or move on. You wait and see."

The wagon soon left San Saba behind, heading east toward the junction of the San Saba and Colorado rivers. The land consisted of gently rolling hills for the most part, with an occasional gully cut by a creek and a scattering of craggily upthrust ridges. The grass was still lush, testament to a wet spring. Clumps of live oaks and pecans dotted the landscape. It was a pretty country, Hank thought, the only country he had ever known. He had roamed these hills with his grandfather, hunting in the brush, fishing in the streams.

It had been quite a while since they had done any hunting or fishing. They seemed to have trouble finding the time for things like that these days. When you grew up, Hank supposed, it was harder for some reason to do the things you enjoyed. Seemed like it shouldn't be that way.

"Grandpa," Hank said slowly, "why don't we do some fishing tomorrow?"

Thomas glanced over at him thoughtfully. "We ain't been fishing in a while," he admitted. "Might be a good way to spend a day for a change, long as we can find a shade tree somewhere on the bank." He grinned. "I remember the first time you hooked one. Couldn't been more than four years old, and you latch on to the biggest catfish I ever saw. Nearly as big as you, boy. You'd never have landed him if your daddy hadn't been there to help—''

Thomas fell silent abruptly as he realized what he was saying, but Hank went on quickly, "Reckon that was when he was home for a visit. I think I remember that catfish.''

"No, you couldn't. You wasn't but four, like I said."

"Maybe, but I remember it," Hank insisted. "I remember Pa holding him up and showing him to me and telling me that I caught him.''

The boy tried not to be bitter about his father, Thomas reflected in the silence. Enos wasn't a bad man. Thomas knew that; after all, he had raised him. But maybe he wasn't cut out to be a father. Some men were like that.

"I think we'll just do that," Thomas said after a time. "I think we'll go fishing tomorrow."

The road they followed was a good one for this part of the country. A few minutes later it led down into the broad valley where the two streams converged. To the east, across the Colorado, was a range of good-sized hills. There were a lot of snakes in those hills, Hank knew, whole nests of rattlers in dark, rocky dens.

"Reckon that's them," Thomas said, pointing to a clump of trees to the left of the road, close to but not right on top of the banks of the San Saba. Hank could see two wagons parked in a clearing in the trees.

"Looks like there's more than just Mr. Reed and Mr. Ordway," Hank observed. "I see several people."

"I do, too," Thomas replied, frowning in puzzlement.

Hank leaned forward and squinted. "I think one of 'em is a woman, Grandpa!"

"There are two women." His old eyes were still keen. "And five men. Quite a group."

As the wagon bearing the coffin pulled up to the clearing and Thomas halted the mules, Hank recognized one of the mounted men as Gus Ordway. The other one on horseback was cut from the same cloth, a lean, hard-featured man who wore a Colt that looked well-used.

One of the other men was a middle-aged Mexican. He got up onto the box of the wagon Reed and Ordway had used the day before. That left Reuben Reed and one other man on the ground. The second man was tall and well-dressed. Reed strode forward to greet Thomas and Hank.

"Good afternoon, Sheriff Littleton." He glanced at Hank. "I see you brought your grandson."

"Had to have some help with this coffin if I was going to get it finished and out here today."

"You didn't tell anyone else, did you? I thought you understood that this affair had to be kept a secret."

"Nobody else knows anything about it," Thomas said, somewhat sharply. He wasn't too happy with the tone of voice that Reed was taking.

"I'm sure Sheriff Littleton understands perfectly well, Reuben," the smooth-faced man spoke up. He came forward and extended his hand. "Allow me to introduce myself, Sheriff. My name is Abner Clayborne, leader of this little group."

Thomas leaned over and shook Clayborne's hand briefly. He said, "Don't look to me like things are too much of a secret, not with this many folks in on them."

Clayborne waved a hand at the group. "All of my associates are highly trustworthy, Sheriff."

Hank wasn't paying a whole lot of attention to what his grandfather and the man called Clayborne were saying. He was looking at the two women sitting on the box of the Conestoga, and he was trying not to stare. The older one was probably the most beautiful female he had ever seen.

The woman saw him watching her and smiled, and Hank immediately felt a surge of embarrassment that made him drop his gaze. He felt warm all over and knew that he was blushing, but there was nothing he could do to stop it. He remembered the kiss that Rose Ellen had given him.

One slightly ironic smile from this woman packed a whole lot more punch, he thought.

The other woman was younger, just a girl, really, and she seemed as shy as Hank. At least she kept her eyes pointed down and didn't meet his gaze. Hank thought there was a resemblance between the two.

Thomas broke into Hank's reverie by swinging down from the wagon and saying, "Come on, boy, let's get this box unloaded."

"If you don't mind, sir, could you put it over in the other wagon?" Clayborne asked. He turned and called, "Ignacio! Come help these gentlemen. You, too, Reuben."

It took only a moment to carry the coffin over to the other vehicle and slide it up into the bed. Yet that effort was enough to make the men carrying it breathe hard because of the oppressive humidity. It was almost like sucking down a lungful of water, Hank thought.

"Excellent!" Clayborne declared, striding forward to slap the side of the coffin. He climbed up next to it and opened the lid, peering inside intently. Thomas stepped up into the wagon and raised the false bottom. Clayborne nodded, beaming his pleasure. "You've done a fine job, Sheriff. Especially on such short notice."

"I was glad to help out the war effort," Thomas said gruffly. "I just hope it fools them Yankee agents who are after your gold. The last thing those Yankees need is good Confederate gold."

"I couldn't agree more, sir."

Hank had wandered over to stand near Thomas's wagon. He couldn't seem to keep his eyes off the women. The older one was starting to look impatient now, and she suddenly said, "We really should be going, Abner."

Clayborne nodded. "Yes, indeed," he said. He glanced over at Ordway and the other man on horseback, and the two of them spurred their mounts up next to the wagons. Clayborne said quietly, "All right, Gus."

Thomas frowned, suddenly sensing that something was very wrong. He glanced over at his wagon, where both rifles were lying in the floorboards. Hank had put his there when they started unloading the coffin. Thomas turned toward Ordway, unsure what to do.

Then Ordway's right hand dipped to the holster on his hip and flashed up holding the pistol. His face expressionless, he squeezed the trigger and shot Thomas Littleton three times in the chest.

Hank stared, unable to comprehend what was happening. He saw the slugs smash into Thomas's body, saw the bright red stains flowering on the white shirt. Thomas was thrown backward by the shots, his legs hitting the sideboards of the wagon. He tumbled out and landed heavily on the ground. His head fell to the side, and a great gout of blood welled from his mouth.

"Grandpa!"

The scream tore out of Hank's throat, and while it still echoed in the clearing, he grabbed for one of the Henrys in the wagon. As his fingers closed on the stock, he saw out of the corner of his eye the other mounted man drawing his gun. The draw was smooth and fast, and Hank knew that his own stunned effort was too slow. He ducked as the man fired, dragging the rifle along with him.

The bullet smacked close by his ear. Hank hit the ground and rolled, levering a shell into the rifle's chamber as he did so. Shouting out his fury, he jerked the trigger and the Henry blasted. He didn't see where the bullet went.

As he came up on his knees, he heard more screaming. The younger girl, the blonde, was staring in horror at Thomas's body. As she shrieked, she started up out of her seat, but her sister wrapped an arm around her and pulled her back down.

Reed had ducked behind the Conestoga as soon as the shooting started. He had a small pistol in his hand now, slipped from a holster under his coat. The Mexican stood nearby, a shocked look on his face, and when he started forward, Reed leveled the little gun at him and barked, "Hold it, Jiménez! You just stay out of this!"

Abner Clayborne still stood tall in the bed of the wagon, next to the coffin, and Hank tried to shift his aim there. Clayborne was the leader. Clayborne was the man who had given the order to kill. Hank was going to kill him if it was the last thing he ever did.

Before he could pull the trigger again, something slammed into his side. He saw muzzle flashes coming from the guns of the two mounted men, and he seemed to hear the boom of shots, but the sound was coming from somewhere far away. He fired again as the world tilted crazily beneath him, pitching him to the side.

His shirt was wet with more than sweat now. He tried to get to his feet as he screamed, "Damn you!" But his legs didn't want to work, and the rifle was so heavy. He thought about dropping it and going to sleep.

A bee buzzed by his head, but he didn't see anything. There was another one, and another. Then a sledgehammer crashed into the side of his head. After that . . .

Abner Clayborne glanced over at the Conestoga. His face was an expressionless mask. Beth Shelby was still screaming. Louise was trying to shut her up, with no success. Finally, Louise lost patience and slapped Beth hard across the face.

"Shut up!" she demanded. "Just be quiet!"

Beth subsided with a whimper. Her eyes were wide and staring and wet with tears as she looked at the bodies.

"Madre de Dios!"

Clayborne heard the muttered exclamation and looked over at Ignacio Jiménez. The Mexican was crossing himself as he prayed. Reuben Reed stood close by, his little pistol still trained on Jiménez.

"I think you can stop worrying about Ignacio, Reuben," Clayborne said. "He's not going to cause us any trouble. Are you, Ignacio?"

Jiménez shook his head vehemently. "No trouble."

"You realize that sometimes certain measures are necessary, don't you, Ignacio?"

"*Si.*"

Clayborne climbed agilely down from the wagon bed and moved over to stand next to Thomas's body. There was a look of surprise frozen on the old man's face. Probably hadn't suspected a thing, but even if he had, it wouldn't have made any difference.

Clayborne gestured at Ordway. "Check the boy."

Ordway spurred his horse over toward Hank, who was sprawled limply on the ground. The side of his shirt was soaked with blood, and his blond hair was now dark red on the right side of his head.

"He's dead," Ordway called. If there was one thing he had confidence in, it was his ability with a gun.

Clayborne looked over at Reed and Jiménez again and jerked a thumb at Hank's body. "Get rid of it."

"You want us to bury him?" Reed sounded surprised.

Clayborne shook his head. "There's not enough time for that. There's a pile of brush over there in that little draw by the river. Dump him there and cover him."

Reed and Jiménez went to Hank. Each man took an arm, and they dragged the body away from the camp while Clayborne went over to the Conestoga. Beth watched him, horrified.

Clayborne paused next to the wagon and looked solemnly up at the women. "I'm sorry you had to see that, Beth," he said softly. "There are a great many unpleasant things we have to face in this life."

"Did you have to do it right in front of her?" Louise hissed. "She didn't have to know."

"You can't continue to shield the child all her life, Louise. Sooner or later she has to learn the harsh realities. I'm sorry about the boy, but it was Littleton's decision to involve him in the matter."

"Y-You . . . you killed them!" Beth shivered.

"There was nothing else we could do, my dear. We have to conceal our trail, and besides, we can put the old man's body to good use."

The callousness of his statement brought on another fit

of sobbing from Beth. Clayborne shook his head in disgust and turned away, leaving Louise to comfort her sister. He called out, "Get those bloody clothes off the old man and dress him in that uniform."

Smith rode over to the back of the Conestoga and reached inside for a package. When he tore off the brown paper, the uniform of a Confederate colonel was revealed. He took the uniform over to Ordway, who was already dismounted and taking Thomas's blood-stained shirt off.

By now Reed and Jiménez had Hank's body nearly to the riverbank. Both men were breathing hard from the effort. The little draw Clayborne had mentioned had been cut in the bank by water runoff when it rained hard, and enough brush had been washed down into it to make a thicket.

Reed pointed at the brush and said to Jiménez, "Make a place for him." Jiménez did as he was told, sliding down the side of the dry draw and pulling some of the brush back to create a little hollow. "Take his feet," Reed ordered. Jiménez grabbed Hank's feet and pulled. The body slid over the side of the draw and started to roll. Jiménez let it bounce down into the space he had made. He bent over and grasped Hank's shoulders, twisted the body, and shoved it down a little more. Then he pulled the brush back over the hollow, effectively concealing the body from casual glance.

That he, Ignacio Jiménez, had sunk so low as to be hiding the corpse of a murdered boy! There had been a time when he wouldn't have dreamed that such a thing was possible. He had known from the start, though, that Clayborne and his group were thieves and quite possibly killers. He should not be suffering an attack of conscience now. There was nothing he could do for the boy and the old man. The only thing he could do was look out for himself.

Reed brushed his hands off as if it had been he who had done the work of climbing down into the draw.

"Come on," he said sharply to Jiménez. "Abner's in a hurry to get moving."

Jiménez clambered up out of the little gully and followed Reed back to the wagons. Ordway and Smith had the old man's body dressed in the uniform. They had cleaned the blood from his face, and as he lay stretched out on the ground he looked like he should be on a battlefield, having fallen leading his men into battle.

"Get the gold loaded," Clayborne said, "then get the old man in the box."

It took less than fifteen minutes to move the gold from the trunk to the false bottom of the coffin. Then it was just a matter of moments for the placement of Thomas Littleton's body over the gold. In the silk-lined coffin, he looked even more like a fallen war hero.

Ordway looked at the body, then spat over the side of the wagon. "He's goin' to start stinkin' in a day or so."

"He'll serve our purposes until then," Clayborne replied. "Reuben and I will take the wagon through San Angelo and stop there long enough to establish our identities before we move on. Then we can rejoin the rest of you and dispose of Sheriff Littleton."

"That'll sure throw Kimbell off our trail," Reed crowed, as if the charade had been his idea.

"I certainly hope so," Clayborne agreed. "I'm rather tired of having the good colonel dogging our heels."

Jiménez summoned up the nerve to ask a question of Clayborne. "The people of San Saba, won't they come looking for their sheriff?"

"Of course, but how will they know where to look? Littleton told no one except his grandson of his connection with us."

"We're ready to roll, sir," Reed pointed out.

"Indeed. Let's get moving, shall we?"

The little caravan pulled out of the clearing, the Conestoga in the lead. Jiménez came next, driving the wagon with the coffin, the gold, and Thomas's body, Ordway riding alongside. Smith brought up the rear in the other wagon.

Ignacio Jiménez cast one glance toward the San Saba River as they left, toward the draw where Hank's body was hidden. He felt a pang of regret as he thought about the boy, cut down at such an early age. Hank had to be dead, shot in the side and in the head like that.

The faint stirrings of a pulse he had felt when he moved Hank's body had to be just his imagination.

Five

Night had fallen in the little town of Eagle Cove, about a hundred miles north and west of San Saba. The lamps were lit in the Mosshorn Saloon, and the place was full. Two bearded oldsters sat on straight-back chairs in one corner and scraped a tune out of their fiddles, providing music for the few couples that wanted to dance. Most of the customers were more interested in gambling or pawing at the painted women or pouring whiskey down their throats.

A man dismounted and tied his horse at the hitchrail along with quite a few others. He paused a moment before going in, letting his eyes adjust slightly after long hours of riding through darkness. His clothes were nothing unusual: boots and jeans and a cotton shirt that had once been white. He wore a black cowhide vest and black leather cuffs on his sleeves, and the big hat on his head was black as well. The high heels of the boots made him tall, and he moved with a lithe, easy grace as he pushed through the batwings of the saloon.

The old fiddlers kept up their scratching and scraping, and the dancers kept whirling around awkwardly. Cards were dealt and money was shoved back and forth across the gambling tables. The clink of bottle against glass went on uninterrupted.

The man walked over to the crowded bar, the clink of his spurs lost in the other sounds that filled the room. There was an opening for a second, and he shouldered into it. He leaned forward, caught the eye of one of the dirty-aproned bartenders, and said, "Beer."

The bartender bent over and drew a beer from one of the barrels, then slid the glass to the newcomer. The glass wasn't too dirty, the man noted. He picked it up and drank thirstily, and when he put it down he found the bartender glowering across the planks at him.

"Customary to pay for it first, friend," the bartender growled.

"Sorry," the man said mildly. He seemed to be naturally soft-spoken. Reaching into a pocket inside his vest, he brought out a coin and flipped it to the bartender, who caught it deftly. More than half the glass of beer was left, and the man sipped it slowly now, his initial dryness blunted.

He turned half around, leaning his left arm on the bar, holding the beer in that hand. The right hand didn't stray too far from the walnut grip of his holstered Walker Colt. His brown eyes scanned the room.

Most of the men here were simple cowhands, poor men who spent what little money they had on basic pleasures. There was also a scattering of gamblers, better dressed for the most part. And there were a few men who looked like cowhands but weren't. The low-slung guns they wore, and the look in their eyes, was enough to tell you that.

Moon Hamilton was one of that last group.

He looked like a badger, small and ugly and mean, with a long-nosed face and a tangle of sandy hair under the battered black hat he wore. He was dancing with one of the saloon girls, twirling enthusiastically and keeping the girl half out of breath. At a nearby table, two more men clapped along with the fiddle music and called out ribald comments as Hamilton let his hand slip down to the girl's rear end. She didn't move his hand, but instead just looked bored. Each man at the table had a girl perched on his lap, and there was a nearly empty whiskey bottle in the center of the table, surrounded by glasses.

Looked like a party was going on in Eagle Cove, the man at the bar thought. Hamilton and his friends wouldn't take kindly to having it interrupted.

He turned back to the bar and crooked a finger to bring the bartender over again. Leaning forward so he could be heard more easily, he said, "That's Moon Hamilton, ain't it?"

The bartender glanced in Hamilton's direction, proving that he knew who the outlaw was, then shrugged. "I don't ask folks for their names, mister. I just pour the booze."

"Just curious."

"That's your problem, friend," the bartender said flatly.

That was the truth. Out here on the frontier, you didn't ask a man too many questions unless you were ready to back them up.

The man finished the last of the tepid beer and set the glass down carefully. The bartender was still standing there, so he said, "I reckon those two at the table are Moon's friends. I hope he ain't got too many more."

The bartender's eyes narrowed in the first show of emotion. "I don't want trouble in here."

"I'll remember that," the man said. He smiled slightly and then stepped away from the bar, making a mental note to keep an eye on the bartender.

He walked slowly among the tables, glancing down at the card games he was passing. Small stakes. There wasn't much money in this whole town. Hamilton and the other two were probably just stopping here long enough to get drunk and buy women.

Why they had stopped didn't matter. What mattered was that he had finally caught up to them.

The table where the other two men sat was the last one in the line of tables. The man stopped about ten feet away from it and stood there for a moment, his thumbs hooked in his belt. After a few seconds, one of the men at the table became aware of his presence and looked up with a scowl. That brought the attention of the other one, who ran his gaze over the newcomer and then said sharply, "Moon!"

Hamilton stopped dancing abruptly and shoved the girl away from him. The men at the table were still seated, but the women deserted them, standing up and moving to the side without wasting any time. The two old men in the corner put their fiddles down.

Now the whole place was suddenly paying attention to the tall, soft-spoken stranger.

Moon Hamilton glared at the man and said, "What the hell do you want?"

"Are you Moon Hamilton?" the man asked quietly, though he knew full well who the outlaw was.

"Who's askin'?"

The stranger turned his left hand around, revealing what he had slipped out from behind his belt—a silver star on a silver circle.

"The Texas Rangers," Enos Littleton said.

From the Red River to the Rio Grande, badmen knew and hated that badge. Hamilton was grabbing for his gun before the words were even out of Enos's mouth.

The Ranger's right hand flashed to his holster, smoothly drawing the Colt in a blur of motion. Hamilton's gun was just coming up level when Enos squeezed the trigger. The pistol blasted and bucked against his hand as Moon Hamilton was thrown back by the slug crashing into him.

His two friends went diving out of their chairs, going in opposite directions. Enos had to make a split-second choice. He pivoted right, triggering again as an outlaw gun boomed. He saw his bullet catch the man in the shoulder and flip him around, and then he was turning, trying to pick up the other one.

A gun went off behind him, and he felt the wind of a slug whipping by his ear. Enos dove for the floor as another shot cracked. He rolled over the rough planks, bumping into the legs of a table, and saw out of the corner of his eye that the bartender he had spoken to was the one firing at him. He snapped a shot in the man's direction, close enough to make him duck, then surged to his feet and tried to locate the two outlaws. Girls were screaming and men trampled on each other as they tried to get out of the way. The Mosshorn Saloon was emptying in a hurry.

Enos ducked behind an overturned table as another shot burned by him. There were only a couple of bullets left in his gun, and with his left hand he punched more cartridges out of the loops on his shell belt. He glanced over the top of the table and saw the second bartender leveling a shotgun at him. Enos dove for his life as the greener roared and the buckshot blew the table to kindling.

He landed hard on the floor and fired without aiming, letting instinct guide him. The man with the shotgun rocked back, dropping the weapon as he clapped his hands to his suddenly bloody chest. He staggered into the shelves holding the saloon's liquor supply, and there was a huge crash and jangle of breaking glass as they collapsed.

Enos's eyes flicked to the back of the room. Somehow Moon Hamilton had gotten back onto his feet, and he was holding a pistol and trying to line it up on the Ranger. His friends, including the one Enos had wounded in the shoulder, were flanking him, also ready to blaze away. Not to mention the remaining bartender, who was drawing a bead on Enos with blood in his eye.

For the first time in his life, Enos wished he didn't keep the hammer of the Colt resting on an empty chamber.

He fired his last shot.

The bullet clipped through the chain holding the lantern at the far end of the bar. It landed on the floor behind the bar with a shattering crash, right in the puddle of spilled liquor. As the flames licked out from the broken lantern, the alcohol ignited with a roar, racing up the length of the bar. The bartender dropped his pistol to slap at his clothes, shrieking as the fire engulfed him.

Enos came to his feet as more bullets sang around his head. Hamilton and his two friends were emptying their pistols at him, and it was a miracle he was untouched as he headed toward the window.

He smashed through the window, a shower of razor-sharp shards falling around him, and landed in a rolling somersault on the ground outside.

There were several little cuts on his face and hands, but he ignored them as he came up onto his feet and started reloading the pistol while running for cover. A glance over his shoulder told him that the dry wood of the saloon's structure had caught fire. It would be an inferno in there in a matter of seconds, but he spotted staggering movement in the shadows and heard ragged coughing. Hamilton and the other two reeled away from the burning building.

Enos called out, "Hold it, Hamilton!"

Hamilton turned, his gun coming up as he searched for the source of the voice. Spotting Enos in the glare cast by the blaze, he shouted, "There he is!"

The crash of guns blended into a long roar like thunder. Enos stood his ground, triggering shot after shot until the Colt was empty again.

Then he walked forward slowly toward the three bodies on the ground.

None of them were moving now. He didn't know if he had hit Hamilton again or not, but if he hadn't, the wound he had inflicted in the saloon was enough to finish off the outlaw. The other two were hit cleanly in the body.

Wearily, Enos thumbed more shells into his gun and

listened to the crackling as the saloon went up in smoke. The roof fell in a moment later with a grinding crash, followed by the walls.

"Hold it right there, you polecat!"

The angry voice came from behind him. Enos still held the pistol in his hand, but instead of spinning around, he turned his head slowly and looked to see who was giving him orders. The man standing there was middle-aged and wore overalls and a disreputable hat, but the light from the fire shone on a badge pinned to his shirt. There was also a rifle in the man's hands, pointed right at Enos's head.

Enos moved cautiously, not wanting to alarm him. He slid the Walker Colt back into its holster, then said, "You the sheriff around here?"

"That's right. And I don't have to ask who you are."

Enos frowned but didn't say anything.

"From the looks of things, you're Beelzebub himself," the sheriff went on angrily. "They told me you were shooting up the Mosshorn. Didn't say anything about burning it to the ground. Where's Buster and Deegan?"

"They were the bartenders?" Enos asked.

"Deegan owned the place as well as tending bar." A look of shocked realization passed across his face. "You don't mean to tell me they're still in there?"

"I'm afraid so. They tried to kill me when I went after Hamilton there." Enos gestured at the outlaw's body.

"Hamilton? Moon Hamilton?"

"That's the one," Enos confirmed.

The sheriff looked thoughtful, but he didn't lower the rifle. "I've seen quite a few reward dodgers on him," he admitted. "What was your grudge against him?"

"No grudge, just my job. I'm a Texas Ranger. Been tracking him all the way from Fort Worth."

The sheriff's eyebrows lifted. "A Ranger, eh? Got any proof of that?"

Enos jerked a thumb at the saloon, where the fire was slowly dying out. Luckily, there were no other buildings close to the rubble, and the assembled citizenry was keeping a close eye on it. Enos saw several men carrying buckets of water in the gathering crowd.

"Afraid I dropped my badge somewhere in there in the excitement," he said. "Ol' Rip Ford'll take replacement costs for it out of my pay."

The name of the Ranger captain evidently struck a chord in the sheriff. "Work for Rip Ford, do you? I knew him awhile back, knew some of his boys. What's your name, mister? Maybe I heard of you."

"Enos Littleton. I rode with Ford against Juan Cortina, then went back in when the war started."

"How come you didn't join the army?" The rifle barrel was starting to sag now, as the sheriff's belief in Enos's statements grew stronger.

"Figured the folks around here would need somebody to help look out for them, especially with so many of the ablebodied men being gone and all. Hasn't been much Indian trouble, but there's been plenty of renegades and outlaws on the prowl. Anyway, I don't cotton to shooting regular folk."

The sheriff lowered the rifle's butt to rest on the ground. "Reckon you're telling the truth," he said. "I know Hamilton was a desperado, and I've suspected for a long time that Deegan's place was a stopover for men on the dodge. Maybe you did the town and the state a service."

Enos lifted a hand to rub tired muscles in his neck and shoulders. "Glad you think so, Sheriff. Now that this ruckus is over, you reckon I could borrow one of the cells in your jail? I've been on the trail a long time, and I could do with a cot to sleep on tonight."

"I can do better than that," the sheriff said, trusting Enos completely now that he had accepted him for a Texas Ranger. "I'll take you back to my place and you can sleep in a bed. Get my missus to fix you a real breakfast in the morning, too."

"A cot in the cell will do right nice," Enos said. "Don't want to be a bother."

"No bother. You come along with me. I'll get somebody to tend to this mess." The sheriff's sweeping gesture took in the dead bodies and the now burned-out saloon.

A bed would feel good, Enos thought. Most of the time he slept under the stars. The last time he had stayed in a bed was on one of his infrequent visits home to see his father and Hank.

As he followed the sheriff, he wondered how the two of them were doing these days.

It was a peaceful night in San Saba, which was good because Sheriff Littleton hadn't been around all evening. Usually he or Hank made the rounds of the town and checked on the various businesses, made certain that there was no trouble at either saloon.

Doc Yantis came out of the Red Top and paused to lean against one of the posts holding up the porch. He pushed his old beaver hat back on his bald head and regarded the main street of town. There were still a few people at Feemster's Mercantile, but other than that everything was closed.

The soft sound of a horse's hooves came floating through the night air. Doc looked down at the east end of town and saw a lone man in the street.

The man walked with a rigid gait that bespoke a military background, though he wore civilian clothes. The horse he was leading had a military saddle, too, but that didn't mean a whole lot, Doc Yantis knew.

In the light from the saloon, Doc saw that the newcomer was tall and broad-shouldered. Though his clothes carried plenty of trail dust, they didn't look too old.

Doc's first thought was that the man was probably a deserter, since he seemed to be in good health and probably hadn't been mustered out due to an injury. He had an eye for that sort of thing. One look at the stranger's face cast doubt on the desertion idea, though. It was a strong face, lean and hawk-nosed and framed by bushy side-whiskers heavily touched with gray. When the man paused and took off his hat to run gloved fingers around inside it and dry off the sweat, a thick head of hair the same shade was revealed.

The man stared at Doc for a long moment, and Doc started to feel a little nervous. He shifted the toothpick in his mouth from one corner to the other. "Howdy, mister," he said. "Something I can help you with?"

"Do you live around here, sir?" the man asked, his voice reminding Doc of a hellfire-and-brimstone preacher.

"Sure do. Been in this neck of the woods all my life."

"I'm looking for some people. Five men and two women. The women are young. They'll be traveling with two wagons."

The words had obviously been spoken many times before. Whatever search mission this man was on, it had been a long one.

"Can't say as I've seen them, mister. Three strangers come into town yesterday mornin' and tried to hold up one of the local saloons, but I don't think they were part of the bunch you're lookin' for."

The stranger leaned forward, an intent look on his face. "Why not?"

"Well, maybe they was, but I hope not, 'cause two of 'em won't be leavin' town." Doc nodded toward the church. "They're down there in the cemetery."

The stranger's interest quickened again. "What happened?"

Doc Yantis told him the story of the attempted holdup and how Hank Littleton had stopped it. He enjoyed his role as storyteller and dressed up the tale with plenty of flourishes. When he was through, the stranger asked, "These robbers, what did they look like?"

Doc shrugged and described the two dead men as best

he could, and he could see the tension leave the man's face.

"It's not them," the stranger said finally.

"Well, mister, I hope you find who you're lookin' for," Doc said. "As for me, it's kind of late and I'm a tired old man. You might ask about your friends inside the saloon."

For the first time, the man smiled. "I'd like to catch up to them, but they're not my friends at all."

The next morning Enos rode down Eagle Cove's only real street, a mess of bacon and biscuits wrapped in paper and stored in his saddlebags. Sheriff Mallick's wife had insisted on feeding him and sending extra for the trail.

Enos wanted to stop at Mallick's office and thank the lawman for his hospitality once more before leaving town. He frowned as he saw a familiar-looking horse tied up in front of the sheriff's office. As he pulled up alongside the animal, he checked out the saddle and the harness and knew who it belonged to. Sure enough, seventeen-year-old Dooley Jaeger came out of Mallick's office with the sheriff and grinned that silly grin.

"You're a pure-dee difficult man to catch up to, Enos," Jaeger said. "I been about two jumps behind you ever since you left Fort Worth."

"What's wrong, Dooley?" Enos asked his fellow Ranger.

Jaeger shook his head. "Don't know." He reached inside his shirt and pulled out a crumpled envelope. "Lieutenant Dalton got this letter right after you left. He read it and sent me after you with it."

Enos pushed his hat back and sighed. His boss at the Ranger station in Fort Worth didn't believe in a lot of wasted time in between assignments.

"At least you rounded up our old friend Moon 'fore I caught up with you," Jaeger went on. "The sheriff here told me about your little dancin' party last night."

"Too bad you weren't here, Dooley," Enos said dryly.

"You would have enjoyed it." He leaned over in the saddle and extended his hand. "Might as well let me see it."

He opened the battered envelope and scanned the note. He quickly picked out the important passages.

CSA REQUESTS WE DISPATCH BEST AVAILABLE MAN TO PICK UP TRAIL OF GROUP WANTED FOR THEFT OF ARMY PAYROLL FROM FORT SMITH. FIVE MEN TWO WOMEN IN GROUP. NO NAMES AVAILABLE. BELIEVED HEADED FOR EL PASO. ALSO DESERTER THADDEUS KIMBELL EX-COLONEL CSA MAY BE INVOLVED. ACT IMMEDIATELY ON THIS MATTER

Enos folded the note, replaced it in the envelope, and slipped it in his pocket. "Dalton wants me on this job?"

"That's what he said," Jaeger replied.

Enos leaned over and shook hands with Mallick. "So long, Sheriff. I appreciate everything you and your wife did."

"Always glad to help out the Rangers," Mallick said, his grip firm. "I'll be seein' you, son."

Jaeger rode alongside Enos on the way out of Eagle Cove, prodding him for the details of the fight with Moon Hamilton and his men. Enos changed the subject by asking, "You headed back to Fort Worth?"

"Reckon I am. Do I tell the lieutenant you're startin' out on the assignment?"

Enos hesitated. He hadn't disobeyed orders yet, but this job was going to interfere with some plans he'd made. "I was planning on swinging by San Saba to see my pa and my boy. It's been awhile. . . . Ah, hell. I'll be heading west, I suppose."

"Figgered you would. Wish I could go with you, but the lieutenant told me to get on back and stay out of the ruckus. Good luck, Enos. Reckon you may need it."

EPITAPH

Enos watched Jaeger take the trail for Fort Worth, thinking that the kid couldn't be much older than Hank. He had been looking forward to seeing Hank and his pa. He could always stop and see them later on, though. Once this assignment was over, then he'd get to San Saba for sure.

Six

The wetness trickling across his face was the first thing Hank felt when consciousness came back to him. His hair was soaked and plastered to his head, and it felt like the left side of his face was lying against sticky mud.

He hurt. He hurt bad. And for long moments, all he could do was lie there and whimper with the pain.

The throbbing in his head was matched by the burning in his side. The flow of water seemed to pound against his skull, and it was increasingly getting into his nose and mouth. The realization that he had to lift his head worked its way into his brain.

The first effort made him gag and retch, but there was nothing in his stomach to expel. The spasms only made the pain in his side worse. But he wasn't going to lie here—wherever here was—and drown.

He forced his muscles to work, got his arms under his body, and heaved himself up. His hands slipped in the mud, but he caught himself before he pitched forward again. Something seemed to be tearing at him and holding him back, and it slowly sank in on him that he was covered with dead brush. He pushed some of it away, but then another bout of nausea hit him and drove him down again.

Once the sickness had eased somewhat, a second try got him up on his hands and knees. He eased his way out of the grip of the brush and looked up, following the slope in front of him. He was in a gully somewhere, and rain was falling. The drops washed the mud from his face as he gazed up at the night sky. The water was cool, and the pain in his head didn't seem quite so bad now.

Several rivulets were coursing down the side of the draw, and Hank knew he ought to get out of there. It was unlikely that the gully would fill with water, not unless it rained a lot harder than it was now, but that possibility existed. He reached out, found handholds, and started trying to crawl up the slope.

The climb was a long nightmare. For every foot of progress he made, it seemed like he slipped down two feet.

Finally, he felt the edge of the draw underneath his fingers. He held on tighter, scrabbled for purchase with his feet, and threw himself over the top to go sprawling full-length in lush wet grass.

He stayed there for another long interval, content just to be alive and breathing. But as he rested, memories began to steal in, bringing with them awful, bloody images.

The blast of guns . . . acrid smell of powder smoke. Bullets thudding into his grandfather's body and flinging him backward off the wagon . . . a girl screaming somewhere . . . the rifle bucking in his grip. . . .

Lightning flickered and thunder rumbled in the distance a moment later. The rain became heavier, and as it struck Hank's face, it mingled with the tears rolling from his eyes.

He had been shot; he remembered that now. At least one bullet had passed through his side, and from the feel of his head he knew that a slug had clipped him there, too. He lifted his hand and tentatively explored the throbbing pain that was his skull. There was a knot there, a goose egg bigger than the one he had gotten falling off the porch when he was eight. When he touched the injury, his head seemed to swell up even larger and become more painful, but that subsided after a moment. He closed his eyes and rested.

When he felt strong enough, he pulled his sodden shirt up and tried to figure out how bad the wound in his side was.

I'm shot, Hank thought. He had known that in his brain, but now the realization hit his gut and exploded into fear and panic. He wanted to scream, to cry out for himself and for his grandfather. Hank gulped down a deep, shuddery breath and tried to force the frenzy of emotion far back into the recesses of his brain. He couldn't do himself or anyone else any good if he lost control.

Neither of his wounds were fatal, he told himself. The chief danger was gangrene, and to guard against that, he had to get back to town, had to find Doc Yantis.

He had to take his grandfather home.

Hank pushed himself up once more, painfully climbing to his feet. That took more out of him than he had expected, and he would have fallen again if he hadn't been able to grab on to the trunk of a nearby cottonwood. The night was as dark as any he had ever seen, but his eyes could pick out a few shapes. He thought he knew where he was. Mixed in with the sound of the rain he thought he could hear running water, and he knew he had to be close to the banks of the San Saba.

Hank held on to the tree, pulling himself together, and while he waited, lightning flashed and told him that he was right. In the split-second glare, he caught a glimpse of the little river.

Lightning began to come more often, and the thunder that followed was louder. The ground quivered under Hank's feet. The main body of the storm was moving over now, with harder rain and stronger wind.

Thomas had been wrong. The clouds had held a storm after all.

Hank sobbed, and he kept crying as he pushed away from the tree and staggered along the bank, looking for his grandfather's body while the lightning flashed. After a while, he seemed almost to forget what he was doing and reeled along mindlessly. A warning voice in the back of his head told him insistently that what he was doing was only going to get him killed. In the condition he was in, if he fell off the bank into the river he would drown for sure. There was nothing he could do for his grandfather now. Thomas had to be dead.

Hank tried to tell himself that if he had lived through the shooting, maybe Thomas had, too. He *knew* better, though. Thomas had been shot several times, solid hits in the body at close range.

Hank turned away from the river, guilt eating at his soul even as he did so. He didn't want to die, but he didn't want to leave his grandfather's body behind.

But, oh God, he didn't want to die. . . .

Doc Yantis lifted his head from his pillow and frowned in the darkness. He thought he had heard something, but now all he could hear was the rattle of rain on the window of his bedroom. He had been sound asleep, and he wondered how long it had been storming. His head sank down, and he closed his eyes.

There it was again, a thumping noise that wasn't being caused by the storm. Doc sat up in bed and listened. A moment later, the sound came again.

Someone knocking on the back door in the middle of the night in weather like this? Well, he *was* a doctor, and it wasn't like this was the first time he had been summoned in the middle of the night.

Doc swung his feet out of bed and padded through the little house in his nightshirt. He heard the thumping noise one more time, and then it fell silent. It had definitely come from the back door, though. Doc went through the kitchen and paused at the door.

"Anybody out there?" he called through the door.

Silence, except for the rush of the rain.

Doc thought about going back to bed, but his curiosity wouldn't let him. He knew he had heard something.

He unlatched the door and started to pull it open slowly. Weight fell against it, pushing it at him. Doc stepped backward quickly.

The door banged open as a body slumped through it and fell to the floor. The man wasn't moving, whoever he was. Doc turned to the counter, found matches and a candle. Rain blew in the open door as he scraped one of the matches into life and held it to the wick.

The feeble glow caught and grew brighter, wavering in the wind from the storm. Doc took a cautious step closer to the body and leaned over. It was Hank Littleton, and just as a gust of wind blew out the candle, Doc saw the bullet wounds on the boy's head and in his side.

"My God," he whispered in the sudden darkness.

Hank wouldn't have believed it was possible to hurt worse than he had the night before, but when he woke up the next morning, he found that it was all too true. When he tried to sit up in bed, his head felt like it was going to explode. Sinking back against the pillow, he couldn't help but let out a groan.

Bed. He was lying in a bed with clean sheets, and the things wrapped around his head and middle were bandages. The night was over, and he was alive.

Hank didn't remember much about the walk into San Saba the night before. What he remembered most vividly was the sight of Thomas falling from the wagon, his shirt suddenly bloody. . . .

The door of the small, spartanly furnished room opened, and Doc stuck his bald head in. "Thought I heard you," he said. He came into the room and stood over the bed, peering intently at Hank. "How do you feel this morning?"

"N-Not g-good." Hank's voice sounded strange to him, raspy and half strangled.

"I'm not surprised. A man shouldn't feel good after being shot a couple of times."

Hank tried to sit up. He said weakly. "Doc—"

"Here now. You just stay still, son. You lost some blood, and you're going to need a lot of rest. Hell, you may even have a concussion, but you're going to be all right. I got the wounds cleaned. Shouldn't be any problem with festering." Doc leaned over the bed. "Now, what about your grandpa, Hank?"

"That's what I wanted to tell you," Hank replied, his voice little more than a whisper now. "He was sh-shot, too. I don't know if . . . I couldn't find him. . . . I've got to get up and go out there, Doc."

"You're not going anywhere," Doc said sternly, his face betraying the worry he felt for Thomas Littleton. "Where did this happen, son?"

"East of here . . . by the river . . . close to the Colorado. . . ."

"I'll send somebody to look," Doc promised. "You get some more rest now."

"Got to help Grandpa—"

Hank fell back, exhausted, unable to fight off sleep any longer.

They came to Doc's house late that afternoon, came to see Hank. Four of San Saba's solidest citizens, all of them with long faces.

Hank was feeling better before they arrived. He had slept a lot of the day, resting his brain, as Doc put it. The broth that Doc brought to him later made him gag at first, but he discovered as he forced the food down that he was truly hungry.

Doc told him that a group of men from town had gone out to look for his grandfather, and Hank had waited anxiously for their return. When Doc showed the four men into the room, though, Hank knew they didn't have any good news.

"We couldn't find him, son," one of the men said. "We found where that camp had been all right, but your grandpa and his wagon weren't anywhere around."

Hank closed his eyes and tried to steady his breathing. "You looked in all the gullies and draws?"

"Sure did. We even searched a long ways downriver. The only sign of Thomas was . . . this."

Speaking quietly, the man held out a bundle of clothes. Moving with a slight awkwardness that could have come from the fact that he was nervous, he unrolled the wet clothes. Hank turned his eyes away when he saw the holes with dark stains around them. "Those are his," he said.

"I was afraid so," the man said. "Don't see how anyone could lose that much blood and live."

"They couldn't," Doc said quietly.

"I sure can't figure out what those fellers did with the body—" The man broke off when he saw Hank's features twist in pain. He turned to Doc and went on in a low voice, "Reckon we'd better go on."

"Yes," Doc agreed. "I think that might be a good idea."

When the men were gone, Doc sat down on a stool next to the bed and said to Hank, "I don't understand any of this, son. I know you're telling the truth about these men, but it surely doesn't make any sense." He frowned in thought now. "There were five men and two women, you say?"

"That's right," Hank said dully.

Doc blinked rapidly. "There was a stranger in town last night," he said. "He was looking for five men and two women, traveling with two wagons. I forgot all about him until now."

"You think he's still in town?"

"I don't know, but if he is, he might be able to tell us

just who those people really are." Doc smiled, but the expression was grim. "I think it's safe to assume they weren't really Confederate agents." He stood up. "You'll be all right here by yourself for a little while. I think I'll go down to the Red Top and see if I can hunt up that stranger."

Hank nodded and leaned his head back on the pillow. He hoped that Doc could find the man, too.

There were a lot of questions to be answered before justice could be done.

The man Doc had talked to the night before was nowhere to be found in San Saba. The bartender in the Red Top vaguely remembered him coming into the saloon and asking a few questions, but no one knew his name or where he had gone.

"So I'm afraid that's a dead end, son," Doc told Hank when he returned to the house, then immediately regretted his choice of words. "I don't know how we're going to find that bunch."

Hank said something in a voice so low that Doc couldn't make out the words. He leaned closer and asked, "What was that?"

"I'll find them," Hank said.

Doc frowned. There was a look in the boy's eyes that he didn't like. "It'll be a long time before you're up to doing anything," he said. "You can stay here with me while you're mending. Thomas and I were friends, and I don't mind looking after you."

Hank didn't reply, didn't meet Doc's eyes. He stared off at the wall, not seeming to see anything.

The pain was still bad, but that wasn't the worst of it, Hank thought. He had been all through it in his mind. Reuben Reed and Gus Ordway—if those were their real names—had come to San Saba and hired Thomas to make that damned special coffin, and all the while they had been planning to kill him.

Cold-blooded murder, that was what it was. It didn't

seem right somehow that Thomas had devoted his life to giving some dignity to a man's passing on, and now he wouldn't even have a decent burial for himself. No headstone with words to remember him by.

Hank would never forget him, though. And he wouldn't rest until Thomas Littleton's killing had been avenged.

Brave sentiments, he thought. And all the while, he was scared. Lord, he was still so scared. He remembered how it had felt when that slug burned through his body, how close he had come to death. The blackness. How could he go right back and face that again?

"My father," he suddenly said with dry lips. "I've got to get word to my father."

Doc nodded. "I thought about Enos. But you know how it is with the Rangers, Hank. He could be most anywhere. I sent a letter to Ranger headquarters in Austin telling him what happened."

Hank had to admit that Doc was right. There was no way of knowing where Enos Littleton was now. Hank wondered for a moment why he hadn't thought of his father before, but the answer to that was fairly simple, he realized.

He hadn't thought of Enos because he wasn't used to Enos being anywhere around. He hardly ever had been while Hank was growing up. Why should now be any different?

"I don't know if you're feeling up to it or not," Doc went on, "but you've got a couple more visitors waiting in my front room. They're mighty anxious to see you."

Hank wasn't sure about having visitors, but from the look on Doc's face, he thought it was a good idea. "All right," Hank said.

Doc left the room and came back a moment later, ushering two smaller figures in front of him. Jimmy Maxwell and Rose Ellen Hobbs both looked worried, and when they saw Hank lying in bed with his head bandaged, their concern grew.

"Oh, Hank," Rose Ellen exclaimed. "Are you all right?"

That seemed like sort of a foolish question to Hank, but he managed to put a smile on his face and say, "I reckon I will be, Rose Ellen."

"Of course he ain't all right!" Jimmy said. "He's been shot! Leave it to a girl to ask a question like that." From the sound of his voice, even though he was sorry that Hank was wounded, he thought the whole thing was exciting. Then he remembered that Hank's grandfather was dead, and his face fell somewhat. "Does it hurt real bad, Hank?"

"Bad enough," Hank answered. He repressed the urge to be curt to Jimmy. The boy didn't have any real sense of what had happened. Hank didn't understand it himself.

"Is there anything I can do to help you, Hank?" Rose Ellen asked. "I could bake you a cake or something like that."

"Hank don't need any cake right now, I'm afraid," Doc said gently. "He's had a lot of shocks to his system; he needs plainer food for a while."

"How about if I bring you your rifle?" Jimmy wanted to know. "Just in case those outlaws come back to get you."

"Reckon they think I'm dead already," Hank said. "I don't think they'll want to come back to this part of the country."

The conversation brought home to Hank just how little he could afford to be lying here wasting time. That bunch of killers would be putting more miles between him and them with every day that passed.

"I appreciate the two of you stopping by," Hank went on. "I'm getting sort of tired now, though."

"You children run along now. You can come back and see Hank sometime later. He won't be going anywhere."

Jimmy and Rose Ellen left after they bid their good-byes to Hank, Jimmy's farewell taking a tough, man-to-

man tone while Rose Ellen seemed to be almost crying.
Both promised to return later.

"Doc, about that last thing you said . . . that I wasn't
going to be going anywhere . . . I've got to."

"Out of the question," he said sharply. "I know you
want to hunt down those men, son, but you're just in no
shape for it."

"I can't help that. There's nobody else but me to do
the job."

"It's not your job to track down killers."

"The hell it isn't," Hank said flatly.

Doc sighed. The boy surely didn't seem like a child
anymore. With all that he had been through in the last
few days, that shouldn't have come as a surprise. The
frontier was a rough place to grow up. Boys often became
men in a hurry. Enos had left home when he was younger
than Hank to find his own life.

"I'm not going to argue with you," Doc said. "Your
health is my responsibility now, and I say you've got to
recuperate for at least two weeks before you can even
think about leaving this house. I'm sorry, but that's the
way it's got to be. And I think it's the way Thomas would
have wanted it."

Hank took a deep breath and closed his eyes. He
wished Doc hadn't put it quite that way. But he had a
feeling Doc was right.

That didn't change anything. Thomas would have
wanted to protect him, but Thomas was gone now. From
here on out, Hank would have to make his own decisions.

Seven

The next couple of days were almost a blank as far as Hank was concerned. He slept most of the time, and when he was awake, he didn't do much but eat the meals that the women of the town sent over. He couldn't keep up with the supply of food, so Doc ate damn well himself. During the second day, Hank began to feel strong enough that staying in bed became difficult. His thinking seemed to clear, too. The initial overpowering surge of grief and anger had diminished, leaving in its place a core of cold fury.

Late that afternoon, while Doc was nodding off in a rocking chair in the corner of the room, Hank tried his legs out. His head felt a little dizzy as he swung his feet out of the bed and stood up, but he was able to keep his balance. He shuffled to the window and leaned out carefully, enjoying the breeze on his face.

Doc had gone to Thomas's house and brought back some clean clothes, and Hank slipped into them now. His boots were there, too, but when he started to bend over to pick them up, the pain and dizziness got worse. Well, this wouldn't be the first time he had gone barefoot.

He opened the door slowly, being as careful as he could not to make a noise that would wake Doc. It took him a moment to orient himself as he stepped out into the hall, but he soon found his way out.

A few minutes later, as he walked down the street, he knew that people were looking at him in surprise. He looked at the hitchrail in front of the Red Top and saw that there were quite a few horses tied there, but there were even more, plus some wagons, in front of the mercantile. That would be the best bet for what he had in mind, he decided.

The babble of voices inside the store fell silent as he stepped inside. Heads swiveled to look at him. Hank had always liked the smell of the store, a musty mixture of spices and tobacco and horse liniment. Now he hardly noticed it, so intent was he on what he was here for.

When all the townspeople in the store were looking at him, he said in a low voice that somehow carried well, "You all know what happened to my grandpa."

Several of the men and women nodded. Hank new everyone here, he thought. Hardworking folks who had been Thomas Littleton's friends.

"Since my grandpa's dead and my father's not here, I reckon I'm the closest thing to a lawman around these parts." Hank didn't like the way that sounded as soon as he had said it. He didn't want these people to think he was taking too much for himself; he wanted their help, not for them to think he was some arrogant kid. There was nothing he could do now but go on. "I can't let those killers get away with what they did. That's why I'm going after them. I could use a posse to go with me."

For a moment, no one spoke. They all just stared at him, and a few of the men swallowed in embarrassment. Finally, Burchell Feemster, the owner of the store, stepped out from behind the counter at the rear of the place.

"Look here, Hank," he began. "We're all as sorry as all get out about what happened to you and Thomas. You know that. But you can't go off chasin' those killers. You'll just get yourself shot up again if you ever find them, which I don't reckon you can now."

"I can find them," Hank said. "Maybe I won't get shot up if I have some help. Grandpa would've done it for you!"

"But dammit, boy," Feemster said peevishly, "we ain't lawmen. Got no business actin' like Rangers or somethin'."

"I was my grandpa's deputy—"

Doc Yantis said angrily from behind him, "If you were, it was unofficial. I thought I told you to stay in bed, Hank. You shouldn't ought to have sneaked off like that. You'll be flat on your back again if you don't watch out."

Hank looked around the room. The faces he saw were sympathetic, but that sympathy didn't extend to helping him. He was man enough to shoot down the town's outlaws, but not man enough to get a town to follow him.

"I guess you're right, Doc," Hank said hollowly. "I might as well rest. Doesn't look like I'm going anywhere."

Hank stared out the window that evening as the stars came out, studying the winking lights against the deepening blackness. Doc had let him stay out of bed for the most part, though he had had to sit in the rocking chair. After they had eaten, Doc checked the wounds and changed the bandages and proclaimed that Hank was healing nicely.

"Did a nice job, even if I do say so myself. You just be patient, boy, and you'll be as good as new before the summer is over."

Good as new? Hank doubted that. Resting and eating weren't going to get rid of what he had suffered.

Now, as he leaned on the windowsill and peered up and out at the stars, the door of the little room opened and Doc stuck his head in. "How you feeling now, son?" he asked.

"I'm all right, I guess."

Doc licked his lips. "Better get on back into bed. I think I'll mosey down to the Red Top for a few minutes."

Hank smiled slightly, keeping his head turned so that Doc wouldn't see the expression. "I'll be fine." There was nothing Doc liked better than drinking a little and socializing a lot, and Hank didn't want to keep him from it.

"I'll look in on you when I get back."

Hank nodded, now knowing if that was meant to be reassuring or a warning. He didn't say anything.

He heard the door of the house close behind Doc, and then he didn't know how much time had passed after that when he heard the door open. Didn't seem like much, though; Doc shouldn't be back so soon.

It wasn't Doc. A female voice called softly, "Hank?"

Hank frowned. It wasn't Rose Ellen Hobbs. The voice was that of an older woman. He said, "In here," and waited where he was.

Dorene Pierson appeared in the doorway. She had a large burlap bag in one hand, and there was a look of concern on her face. Hank realized when he saw her that she hadn't been by to visit before. Thinking about that now seemed strange, since he knew that she and his grandfather had been good friends, but with so much going on, he hadn't missed her.

"Hello, Mrs. Pierson," he said.

"How are you, Hank?"

He nodded. "I'm all right, I guess. I'm a lot better than I was a couple of days ago. Doc says I'll be fine."

"I'm . . . sorry . . . about what happened." The concern on her face was joined by a look of anger. "I heard about what you did in the general store this afternoon. I thought you'd find at least one man in this town."

Hank shrugged. "Can't blame them, I guess. It's not their fight. He was *my* grandfather."

"And he was special," Dorene said softly. "I just can't bear to think about those men getting away."

"Doesn't seem to be much we can do about it."

Dorene smiled sadly. "It looks like there's only one man who can do something. *You,* Hank." As he looked at her in surprise, she opened the bag and reached into it, bringing out a coiled shell belt and holster. The pearl-handled butt of a Remington revolver caught the dim light from the lamp and reflected it. "I want you to have this, Hank," Dorene went on.

His eyes widened even farther. "Where did you get that?" he couldn't help but ask.

"It would have belonged to a . . . to a man I knew once. He was very good with a gun." The enigmatic little half smile on her face hinted at quite a story. "I was going to give it to your grandfather. I'm giving it to you now."

He reached out and took the belt and holster from her, let the palm of his right hand slide over the smooth surface of the Remington's grip. "You're not going to try to talk me out of going after them, are you?" he asked softly.

Dorene shook her head. "I'm going to ask you to go with my blessing and kill those bastards who—"

Her voice broke and she had to turn away for a moment. When she faced him again, her eyes were glistening. "I know it's awful of me to ask you to go after a bunch of killers like that. You're not well. . . ."

"Well enough," Hank replied tautly.

"But they have such a big lead already. If they're ever going to be brought to justice—"

"I know. I thought the same thing. And you're right; there's nobody else to do it."

She reached out tentatively, put her hand on his arm, and squeezed. They had been friends before, but now there was a bond of another sort forming between them. "I've got a couple of horses outside," she said.

"Two horses?"

"I'm going to ride with you a little ways. Thomas said you could shoot the wings off a gnat at a hundred yards with a rifle, but you'd never shot a handgun much. I think I can give you a few pointers, once we get out away from town."

Hank nodded. "All right."

"One more thing." Dorene reached into the bag again. "You'll need money."

Hank started to shake his head, but she pressed the small pouch on him. "Take it," she insisted. He did.

They went together out of the house. Dorene's horses were tied to a tree in Doc's backyard. She took the smaller of the two and swung up into the saddle like a man. Hank wasn't sure what to make of her. He had thought of her as just another middle-aged widow lady, but evidently there was a lot more to her than that. He should have suspected as much, knowing how Thomas had felt about her. He felt a slight pull on his wounded side as he climbed aboard the other horse, but it wasn't enough to worry about.

He started to put the spurs to the horse when Dorene suddenly reached out and caught his arm again. "Wait," she said. "This is wrong. My God, I'm a good Christian woman now. I shouldn't be sending a boy on a mission of vengeance like this. Please, Hank, just forget everything."

Hank looked at her for a long moment, then said, "Right or wrong, I've got to do it. It's not your fault, Mrs. Pierson. I'd be starting down this trail sooner or later."

She listened to his words, sighed, grimaced, and jerked her horse's head around.

The time for thinking was over now, and Hank was glad of it. It was time to take action.

They rode out of San Saba, not stopping until the lights of the town were long out of sight. Then Dorene reined in and said, "This should be far enough that no one will hear the shooting."

They got off the horses and tied the reins to mesquite

trees. There was a nearly full moon floating in the sky overhead, and the light from it and the stars made the rolling landscape fairly bright.

"Wish it was daylight," Dorene said. "We'll make do, though." She put her hands on her ample hips. "Let me see you draw that gun."

Hank reached for the butt of the Remington and started to yank it out of the holster the way he thought a fast gun should. The pistol slipped from his fingers and thumped to the ground instead.

Dorene shook her head. "It takes a long time to make a shootist, Hank, and that's not what we're after here. We just want you to be able to use a handgun if you have to. Now pick it up and check the barrel and the action for dirt."

Hank did as instructed and then slipped the gun back in the holster. "Slower this time, right?"

"That's right," Dorene said.

Hank drew the gun and brought it up, his thumb reaching somewhat awkwardly for the hammer to cock it. He let the hammer back down, reholstered the pistol, and tried the maneuver again. After several tries, the Remington was coming out of the holster fairly smoothly, and he was able to thumb-cock the weapon quickly.

"Now pick a target," Dorene told him.

Hank looked around and saw a little rocky outcropping on the side of a hill about twenty yards away. There were several rocks the size of his fist lying on top of the ridge. Hank took a deep breath. His nerves were strung a little tighter now for some reason. Instead of letting his nervousness get any worse, he pulled the gun and fired quickly, without aiming.

The bullet whined off into the night without hitting anything.

Hank shook his head in disgust and reached over with his left hand to rub his right wrist. The Remington had quite a kick to it.

"You're still trying to take everything too fast," Dorene told him. "The important thing is to aim, and to hit what you aim at."

Hank glanced over at her. "Where'd you learn so much about gunfighting?"

Dorene laughed. "I know more about more things than you'd ever guess, boy."

They worked together for a half hour, and by the time they were done, Hank's wrist ached even more and his ears were ringing under the assault of the black-powder blasts. His wrist would become stronger with time and practice, though, and he might even get used to the noise in time. The important thing was that he could draw, aim, and fire with reasonable accuracy in just under two seconds. That was slow, damned slow, and he couldn't even do that every time, but he didn't feel like a complete novice anymore.

"You keep practicing, you'll get better," Dorene said. "But there's the Henry from the sheriff's office in your scabbard along with a box of ammunition in the saddlebag. Use the Henry whenever you can. Thomas always said you had a natural talent with it, and only a fool neglects what he's naturally good at."

"I'll remember that."

"I'm still not sure about this."

"I am," Hank said. "I've got to at least try."

Dorene nodded. "All right. . . ." Suddenly, she stepped over to him and put her arms around him, hugging him tightly for a moment. "You take care," she whispered.

"I'll be fine," he assured her. "Grandpa always taught me how to take care of myself."

"I know he did." Dorene smiled. "He thought you were pretty special, Hank. I do, too."

She let him go. He hoisted himself into the saddle and grinned down at her. "Nice night for riding," he said.

"It is, isn't it? Good-bye, Hank. *Vaya con Dios.*"

"So long, Mrs. Pierson." Hank swung his horse around and heeled it into an easy lope, its nose pointing west. He didn't look back.

Eight

San Angelo was just a sleepy little cowtown, but as he and Reuben Reed drove the wagon down its main street, Abner Clayborne thought that it would do.

They had left the rest of the group five miles out of town. Ignacio Jiménez was driving the Conestoga now, Thomas Littleton's wagon already having been ditched in a deep ravine. Gus Ordway and Bob Smith were still on horseback and would lead the bigger wagon around the town. The plan called for Clayborne and Reed to rejoin them approximately five miles the other side of San Angelo.

In the meantime, the two of them would set about making sure their effort so far would not be wasted.

They had been three days on the trail from San Saba, and the usefulness of Littleton's body was quickly waning. Soon no one would accept their story about taking their uncle home for burial. The body could be disposed of as soon as they were well out of San Angelo, though.

"Looks like a nice little town," Reed observed as he guided the team down the street. "Wonder how much money they keep around here."

Clayborne chuckled dryly. "Why, Reuben, you're becoming a regular outlaw in your thinking. We don't want to draw too much attention to ourselves."

"I wasn't planning on trying anything."

"See that you don't." Clayborne's voice was harder.

Reed didn't say anything else. He concentrated instead on guiding the wagon to a stop in front of a general store. The place looked fairly busy, and there were several men lounging on the sidewalk. The coffin in the back of the wagon drew interested looks from them.

"We'll buy some more supplies, then perhaps go over to the saloon for a drink," Clayborne said in a low voice. "I'll handle most of the talking."

"Sure, Abner," Reed replied. He was used to Clayborne taking charge.

The men got down from the wagon and walked up onto the sidewalk. It was still hot, and the shade as they stepped under the awning was welcome. Clayborne nodded pleasantly to the loafers and then led the way into the store.

It was like all the other general stores Clayborne had ever seen: cluttered, crowded, and a bit dusty. A long counter ran along the back wall, and customers lined up to give their orders to the clerk. Clayborne patiently waited his turn. Good manners were important, and so was putting up a pleasant front. He prided himself on the fact that people rarely knew what he was really thinking and feeling.

God, he hated all of them.

He suddenly became aware that someone was speaking to him. He glanced up to see a quizzical look on the face of the clerk behind the counter.

"What was that, my good man?" Clayborne asked.

"I asked if I could help you, sir." The clerk was a young man who looked like he should be out plowing a field somewhere instead of working in a store. He looked even more like he should have been wearing a uniform, and Clayborne wondered why he wasn't.

"Yes, you certainly can help me," Clayborne said. "I need twenty-five pounds of flour, a side of bacon, five pounds of coffee, and a couple pounds of sugar. . . ."

Clayborne continued giving his order, the clerk frowning in concentration as he tried to remember all of it. Finally, when Clayborne was finished, the clerk straightened up from his position leaning on the counter. He walked along the shelves lining the back wall, gathering the items. With every other step there was a thump, and Clayborne leaned far enough forward to see that the clerk's right leg had been replaced with a thick wooden peg.

That explained why he wasn't in uniform.

Clayborne looked over at the man who was getting some nails from a barrel. Though the man wore work clothes, he had the look of a solid citizen about him. Just the kind of man Clayborne wanted to talk to, in fact.

The man glanced up and met Clayborne's gaze. He nodded and spoke first. "Howdy, mister."

"Hello," Clayborne said, smiling. He didn't say anything else, wanting to draw the man out. He knew that strangers probably weren't very plentiful and that the locals would be anxious for conversation and news.

"Just passin' through town?" the man asked.

"That's right."

"Got business around here?"

"Unfortunately, yes. My brother and I are taking our uncle home to be buried."

"That's too bad. Where you headed?"

"Bender's Bluff," Clayborne replied, naming a small community a day's journey farther west. He knew it only as a name on a map, and he hoped that this man wasn't overly familiar with the area or its inhabitants.

"Your uncle an old man, was he?"

Clayborne shook his head. "Not that old. He was an officer in the Confederate Army. Died from wounds he received in battle." The story would hold up, he knew, except under extremely unlucky circumstances. The uniform in which Thomas Littleton was laid out was actual Confederate Army issue, and if they were forced to open the coffin, no one would be able to say that Littleton wasn't an actual Rebel colonel.

Clayborne had to repress the slight smile he felt coming on when he thought about how they had obtained that particular uniform. That was one more grudge for Colonel Thaddeus Kimbell to hold against him, he supposed.

Thaddeus Kimbell ate his lunch in the saddle, as usual gnawing on jerky and hard biscuits as he rode. He could have stopped for a hot meal, but every minute wasted was another minute that lying bitch and her friends could gain ground on him. He wasn't going to tolerate that.

God, Texas was hot in the summer! He was from Tennessee, and the country looked like heaven in comparison with this dry, dusty wilderness. Even Arkansas was an improvement on Texas; at least it had the Ozarks. Some cool, forested mountains would be a welcome change.

No matter how high the temperature rose, though, it couldn't be any hotter than the flame of vengeance burning inside him. He had made the mistake of trusting a woman, of surrendering to the passion she aroused in him with her gentle touch and her soft, pliant body. And in the end he had discovered that it had all been a sham. She had gotten the information she wanted from him, and her associates—accomplices might be a better word— had done the rest. The Confederate Army had lost a fortune in gold, and several of his troops had lost their lives. Worst of all, he had lost his rank, his dignity, his self-respect.

Thaddeus Kimbell could not allow that to go unpunished. Rather than face the disgrace of a court-martial, he had accepted the greater disgrace of desertion. It would be worth all the pain, though, when he caught up with Louise Shelby and Abner Clayborne. Then they would pay. By God, would they pay!

EPITAPH

* * *

There was nothing like living out in the open, Enos Littleton thought. Nothing could compare with bacon and beans and panbread cooked over an open fire, and few beds were better than blankets spread out under the stars. Oh, it was all worth it. Maybe he was crazy for being that way, but he got to feeling cooped up when he was in town for too long.

He let the campfire burn down and sat with his back propped against a good-sized slab of rock. The light from the fire was enough to make out the words in the letter he took from his pocket.

Since starting on this job a couple of days earlier, he had thought long and hard about the contents of the letter. It really didn't give him much information. On the face of it, the job seemed impossible. To try to pick up the trail of a small group crossing Texas. . . . Well, he would have to rely in large measure on pure damned luck. Texas was a big place, and he could miss them by a mile a hundred times and never know it.

He wondered where this Colonel Kimbell figured into it. Ex-Colonel Kimbell, that is. Perhaps he had been involved in the payroll theft. It would take something that scandalous to make an officer desert, Enos thought. The letter made it sound like he wasn't part of the gang that had stolen the money, though.

Enos wasn't going to rack his brain anymore about it. He folded the telegram and slipped it back into his pocket. There would be time to ponder the whole situation later.

Nine

Hank stayed in the saddle nearly all that first night, riding west until the sky started to lighten behind him. Then he found a nice spot in a little bowl between two hills and made camp. He didn't start a fire, since he wasn't hungry. The weariness he felt deep in his bones was what he needed to take care of. He tied the horse where there was plenty of grass and then spread his blankets underneath a big live oak. Stretching out never felt so good.

When he woke up, the sun was high in the sky and his side was stiff and sore. For a moment, as he sat up and rubbed his eyes, the urge to go back to San Saba was strong. He had been seriously wounded. He had no business taking off after the killers like this. If he didn't do it, though, no one would.

He could look after the wounds just as well as Doc could, he told himself. The knot on his head had just about gone away, and the gash there was scabbed over and healing up. The wound in his side was a different story. Hank was sure he could handle its care, though.

It was only when he got up that he realized he hadn't

brought anything to eat. Dorene had given him money, but he couldn't eat that. Hank closed his eyes for a moment, thinking that at this rate, he wasn't going to be much of a threat to Abner Clayborne and his men.

There was a small stream nearby, and Hank settled for a long drink of water. It didn't do much for his hunger, but at least his mouth wasn't cotton-spitting dry anymore. He thought the stream was Brady Creek, and if that was the case, he could follow it to the town of Brady, over in the next county. Or maybe it was this county now; as much as he had ridden during the night, he might be out of San Saba County.

He had a feeling Doc had been angry last night when he got home and found his patient gone. Hank frowned as a thought suddenly occurred to him. Would Doc come after him or send someone else after him? The way he saw it, he was on his own now. The only person he might have to answer to would be his pa, and Hank knew how unlikely that was.

Hank rode along beside the creek, trying to figure out how he should go about tracking the killers. Reed had said they were headed for El Paso, but he could have been lying about that the way he lied about everything else. If they were heading for Mexico, there were a lot of other places where crossing the border was easy. They could have gone south, to Eagle Pass or Del Rio. They could go over the border anywhere, Hank supposed, but he had a feeling that they would choose a town. Clayborne hadn't seemed the type to strike out into a complete wilderness.

That was placing a lot of faith in his skill as a judge of character, Hank realized, more faith than was justified by the evidence. He was green, and he knew it. But at least he was doing something.

He was glad he had listened when his pa made a rare visit and talked about his assignments. Being a Ranger had taken Enos all over the state of Texas, and Hank knew a little more geography than might be expected from a boy who had never been more than seventy miles away from home. In every town or village he came to, he would ask about the men he was chasing. If he made it to El Paso without having any luck, he would start working his way back along the Rio Grande.

It was possible he was facing years of searching, and he knew that. He wasn't going to give it up, though, no matter how unsure of himself he was.

He rode on toward Brady, reaching up every so often to scratch at the area around the bandages on his side. The wound was itching and burning a little bit, but Hank was sure it was nothing to worry about.

Hugh Whitfield was the mayor of San Saba as well as the owner of Whitfield's Freight Line, and he was in his company's big barn when Doc Yantis came looking for him. A large, red-faced man, Whitfield was helping one of his hostlers hitch up a wagon team when Doc stuck his head through the open double doors. "Talk to you a minute, Hugh?" Doc asked.

"Just a second, Doc." Whitfield and his helper got the rebellious mules in harness, then the mayor walked over to Doc, brushing off his hands as he did so. "Now, what can I do for you?"

"I guess you heard about what young Hank Littleton did yesterday afternoon?"

"You mean about trying to get up a posse in Feemster's store?" Whitfield nodded. "I heard. Sounds like the boy's got plenty of sand."

"Well, he don't have plenty of sense, that's for sure," Doc replied tartly. "He's gone and run off."

Whitfield frowned. "You think he's gone after them men?"

"That'd be my guess."

"Well, I'm sorry to hear that, Doc," Whitfield shrugged. "Don't know what I can do about it."

"I think somebody ought to go after him."

"If you mean somebody official, nobody around here

84

fits that description anymore. The county's going to have to appoint a new sheriff, but I don't know who they'll get. Hank was the best possibility, even though he's a little young."

"Then what are we going to do?" Doc demanded. "Just let him go off and die?"

"Now, Doc, he's not going to find those men, and you know it."

"Not talking about them. The boy was wounded. One of the wounds was festerin'. He could die on the trail."

"I didn't know that. But I still don't know what I can do about it." Whitfield put his arm around Doc's narrow shoulders. "Look, Doc, I'm not trying to be hardhearted. Lord knows I don't want any harm to come to Hank. But neither one of us, nor anybody else in town, can take responsibility for him. He's a man now and we don't have the right to drag him back from what he wants to do."

"Don't want to take the trouble, you mean." Doc pulled away angrily from Whitfield. "I'd start after him by myself if I wasn't so damned old and useless. When that boy dies, Hugh, I'm telling you . . . it's on all of our heads."

Sure enough, the creek led Hank into Brady. The town was smaller than San Saba, but it had a store, and that was all Hank wanted to see at the moment. He swung down from the saddle and tied the horse at the rail, the burning in his side a little more insistent now. When he went inside carrying the Henry, he got several curious looks.

There were about half a dozen people in the store, including the clerk, who wasn't waiting on anyone at the moment. He was a young man in his twenties, with dark hair slicked down tight against his skull and the beginnings of a mustache.

"What can I do for you, boy?" he asked with a grin.

Hank didn't care for the tone of voice or the fact that he was being called boy by someone two inches shorter than he was. He wasn't here for trouble, though, just for something to eat.

"Need a canteen, some jerky, bacon, flour. . . . Whatever I'll need for quite a while on the trail," he said, well aware of the fact that he didn't *know* everything he'd need on the trail. Once again, the enormity of what he was doing came home to him.

"Goin' travelin', are you, sonny?" the clerk asked, still grinning. "Well, you just hang on. Ol' Lester'll fix you right up." He started gathering up supplies and piling them on the counter. As Hank watched the pile grow, he became aware of the smiles that the other customers were trying to hide. He tried to ignore them as he lifted his free hand to rub his eyes. His head had started to feel a little strange and achy.

"I think that's enough to hold me for a while," he said to the clerk.

"Aw, no, you got to have more supplies than that," the clerk laughed. "You don't want to run out on the trail, now do you? Ol' Lester knows about this stuff, I'm tellin' you." He added another bag of sugar to the stack.

Hank felt his control slipping away from him. He wanted to lean across the counter and smash the rifle butt into the clerk's smirking face. Instead he lined the barrel on the man's chest and said coldly, "That's enough."

The clerk stopped in his tracks, the grin dropping off his face like a rock. Hank heard muttering behind him and knew that the townspeople saw what was happening. He didn't care.

"Here, boy! What the hell you think you're doin'?" the clerk exclaimed. "Is this a holdup?"

Hank shook his head. "No holdup." He held the Henry with his right hand and reached into his shirt pocket with the left, bringing out the small bag Dorene had given him. He laid some money on the counter as sweat popped out on his forehead from the effort of holding the rifle steady. "I can pay. But I only want what I need."

"Well, that's what I was tryin' to give you—" the clerk began in a whining voice.

Hank cut him off with a shake of his head. "You were having some sport with me, mister, and I ain't got the time or the inclination. Now you bag up what I need, charge me for it, and give me my change, if I've got any coming. I've got places to go."

"All right, all right," the clerk muttered angrily.

Hank glanced to the side, where several shaving mirrors were hung up on hooks. He saw one of the customers, a burly young man who had been the one having the hardest time hiding his laughter a moment earlier, coming up quietly behind him.

"And some chewing tobacco, too," Hank told the clerk. He added, "And if your friend jumps me, this rifle's probably going to go off while it's pointed right at you."

The clerk looked up, eyes wide with alarm, and yelled, "Back off, Hubert, you dumb bastard! Can't you see this kid's crazy?"

For the first time since entering the store, Hank smiled. "That's right, mister," he said.

The clerk finished putting supplies into a burlap bag. He handed it over the counter to Hank, then picked up the money. "Would've come to a little more'n this," he said in a surly voice, "but we'll call it square."

"I appreciate that," Hank told him, and meant it. He backed out of the store, keeping the rifle ready if he needed it. No one bothered him, though. In fact, several of the customers looked vaguely embarrassed now, as if they regretted going along with the clerk's joke.

Hank tied the bag of supplies onto the saddle and mounted up, waiting until he was moving off down the street before he slid the rifle back into the boot. He was glad to leave Brady behind him, and he waited until he was well out of town before stopping to dig into the bag and get something to eat.

He followed the creek west. This was all new territory

to him. He knew that San Angelo was somewhere west of here, and figured he'd run across it if he continued in the same direction. He was already kicking himself for not asking back in Brady if anyone had seen a couple of wagons passing through in the last few days. The obnoxious clerk had shaken him up, making him forget the whole purpose of his journey. He would have to learn to control his temper and keep his mind on his objectives if he was going to have any chance of finding the man.

He would ask in San Angelo. He'd make a point of that.

For now, his primary concern was to cover more ground. He tried not to worry about the pain in his side and the headache he had developed.

When he stopped for the night he'd make a poultice from the chewing tobacco. That was why he had bought it in the first place. He had heard enough war veterans tell about making poultices from their chaws when they were wounded. It was supposed to be good for festers, and that was what Doc had said was the greatest danger from the wounds.

He kept the horse moving, following the creek, heading west.

It took him three days of steady riding to reach San Angelo. During that time he kept a chewing-tobacco poultice tied on the wounds in his side, where the bullet had gone in and out, and they seemed to be getting better. They didn't feel nearly as hot and sore now, and his head didn't hurt as much. Looked like old-fashioned remedies were the best.

He still had enough provisions to last awhile, but he decided to restock in San Angelo anyway. Also he'd found that ol' Lester had forgotten to get him a pan for cooking.

San Angelo looked good as he rode down the street in the early evening. It was just a dusty little cowtown, but there were people there. He hadn't seen many people since leaving Brady and hadn't talked to any of the travelers he had seen in the distance. He wasn't used to such solitude, he supposed. Always before he had had his grandfather for company. Thomas always knew how to cheer him up, how to stir his interest with a story or two about the early days of Texas. Many evenings had been spent listening to Thomas tell about the times when he rode with Captain Jack Hays.

Hank felt the hot sting of tears behind his eyes as he remembered those evenings. He supposed it was natural enough that his father had become a Ranger. Enos had grown up with Thomas's stories, too.

He reined up in front of a store and dismounted. As he tied the horse and went up the steps onto the sidewalk, he hoped that he didn't have the same trouble here that he had had in Brady. Some people just automatically assumed that they could make fun of a kid and get away with it. Hank wasn't going to stand for that. He was doing a man's job and he was bigger than most. Had to be the lack of face hair that gave him away. He wished the blond, almost invisible fuzz that had sprouted would turn into the real thing.

His worries came to nothing in this case. None of the customers in the store paid much attention to him, and the clerk who waited on him was more interested in the color of his money than his age. He bought what he judged he'd need, added to his own supplies, and then went back out.

Hank stood with the sack of supplies in one hand and the Henry rifle in the other and looked up and down the street. There was a saloon across the way, and Hank found his gaze returning to it.

He had just been thinking a few minutes before that he was a man now. Maybe he should start acting like a man in other ways. He was thirsty, and he decided on impulse to go across there and get himself a beer.

This wouldn't be the first time he had tasted beer. He and Jimmy had unloaded some kegs for Mose Duncan one day, taking them from a wagon and storing them in the back room of the Cougar Saloon. Actually, he had done most of the unloading, but Jimmy served as lookout while Hank tapped one of the kegs. Mose was busy up in the front room, and both boys figured he would never know the difference. They had sampled the bitter stuff and pretended to like it, but actually it made Hank sort of queasy. It would be a lot better cold, he decided.

It wasn't until a week later, when he overheard a conversation between his grandfather and Mose, that he found out the saloon owner knew perfectly well what he and Jimmy had been doing. Thomas and Mose had had a good laugh over that, especially when Mose described how green around the gills Hank was when he left.

Hank had to chuckle a little bit now at the memory. It still hurt to think about his grandfather, but there were a lot of nice moments stored away in his mind, and Hank knew somehow that it would be a mistake to try to force them away.

The chewing tobacco was in his pocket, and as he walked across the street he thought about taking a chew to make himself look older. He decided against it, though, recalling how he gagged when he had to chew the stuff to make the poultices. Mixing 'baccy with beer didn't sound like such a good idea, no matter how many old-timers did it.

The Bulldog Saloon was one of the largest buildings in town, an imposing false-fronted structure with the establishment's name emblazoned proudly across the fake second story in bright red letters. As Hank went inside, he realized immediately that this was a completely different kind of place than the friendly little Cougar and Red Top.

The Bulldog was crowded, and loud, raucous laughter came from the cowboys who stood along the bar or sat at the scattered tables. There were a few hands of poker in progress, but the main diversions seemed to be drinking and horsing around with the saloon girls, who were wearing low-cut gowns. Every few seconds, it seemed, one of the girls would squeal as a callused hand strayed where it wasn't supposed to. The long bar that ran down the right side of the room was polished mahogany and must have cost the owner a pretty penny. Behind it was a sparkling array of liquor bottles, and on the wall was the most spectacular sight Hank had ever seen—a painting of a somewhat overweight nude woman reclining on a sofa, her long red hair strategically arranged.

Hank stood just inside the batwings and took it all in, his mouth open and his intention to act grown-up forgotten.

It was the wickedest place he had ever seen, with sin floating in the air along with the smoke from innumerable quirlies.

He walked over to the bar, winding around through the crowd, and leaned the Henry against the mahogany. He dropped the sack of supplies at his feet, where he could hold one boot against it and keep track of it. Placing his palms on the bar, he waited until one of the bartenders came to take his order. The man wore a white shirt, a checkered vest, and sleeve gaiters, and he was a dandy sight.

"What'll it be?" he asked, swabbing the bar in front of Hank with a wet rag.

"B-Beer," Hank said, mentally cursing the way his voice sounded, its tentativeness and the way it broke.

The bartender narrowed his eyes. "You sure?"

"I'm sure," Hank said, more firmly now. Even if the man refused to serve him, at least he hadn't called him son.

The bartender shrugged. He got a mug from under the bar and filled it from a keg on the back bar. When he turned back around and placed the mug on the bar in front of Hank, he said, "That'll be four bits."

Hank nodded and took a coin from his pocket. He slid it across the bar and watched it vanish, then picked up the foaming mug. Some of the foam dripped on his hand as he lifted the drink to his lips. A man didn't sip his drinks, he thought. He opened his mouth and drank heartily, his throat working as he swallowed. When he put the mug down, he wiped the sleeve of his left arm across his mouth, the way he had seen other men do.

"Mighty nice after bein' on the trail, ain't it?" the bartender asked.

"Damn right," Hank replied. "You mind if I ask you a question?"

"Go ahead."

"Have you seen anything of a group traveling with two wagons? I think there'd be five men and two women."

The bartender shook his head and wiped with the rag some more. "Don't recall seeing them," he said. "Friends or relatives of yours?"

"No," Hank said. He didn't offer anything further, and the bartender just shrugged. He was used to such things.

Actually, the beer was a lot better cold than hot, but it was still bitter, Hank thought. Well, eventually he'd move up to whiskey. That was a *real* man's drink.

The bartender moved on to wait on someone else, and Hank was left to nurse the beer by himself. He didn't want to drink it too fast, because that would make him drunk. He didn't think he could afford to be drunk. Resting his left elbow on the bar, he turned half around so that he could look the place over some more.

Maybe on closer inspection the place wasn't so glamorous as he had first thought. The paint was peeling on the walls. The elegant gowns of the saloon girls were pretty worn, and some of them had definite marks of age. The same could be said about the females wearing them. He finally moved his gaze on to the poker games, where men in frock coats and vests dealt the cards with swift, effortless motions. Most of the players were cowhands, but the biggest stacks of money were always in front of the professionals. Somehow that didn't surprise Hank. He had heard his grandfather talk about card sharps many times. In fact, Thomas had taught him some of the things to watch out for.

One of the cowhands at a nearby table threw down his cards in disgust as the gambler next to him raked in another pot. "That's enough for me!" the puncher declared as he stood up. "I'm out of this game."

"If that's the way you feel, friend," the gambler said smoothly. He glanced up and saw Hank watching him. He raised his voice slightly and asked, "What about you, young man? Feel lucky tonight?"

Hank smiled slightly and shook his head. "No, thanks, mister. I don't have enough money to throw it away."

The gambler's eyes got a hard look about them. "Are you merely being prudent, friend, or are you casting aspersions on my honesty?"

"I'm saying I don't feel like playing poker right now, and that's all I'm saying." Hank used the weariness he was feeling to let an edge creep into his voice. He didn't want trouble, but he didn't want the man thinking he was scared, either.

The gambler nodded. "A sound answer, and one I accept most readily." He turned back to the table. "Shall we continue, gentlemen?"

When Hank looked around, he found the bartender standing near him again, a thoughtful look on his face. "I'm glad you had the sense not to get in that game, kid. I think it would have been too much for you."

Hank nodded and said, "I think you're right. Does that gambler work for the house?"

The bartender looked over Hank's shoulder at the table and shook his head. "He gives the owner a cut of his profits, but he don't work for the Bulldog. Why?"

"You try to run honest games?"

"You bet we do. This place has a clean reputation."

Hank's voice was so low that only the bartender could hear it. "You might want to tell your boss that that fella is marking the cards, then. You check that big fancy ring he's wearing. It's got a little stud on the inside of it to make the nicks.''

The bartender looked dubiously at him. ''I'd say your imagination is runnin' away with you, kid.''

''Think what you want to.'' Hank drained the beer. ''Just thought I'd be friendly and tell you about it.'' He had spotted the card marking as soon as he saw the gambler dealing. Mose Duncan had kicked a man with a similar ring out of the Cougar one night, and Thomas had told the man to get out of town.

The bartender gestured at the empty mug. ''You want another?''

Hank shook his head. ''No thanks. One's enough.''

He reached down and picked up his sack of supplies and the rifle, then headed for the door. He was halfway there when another man shouldered through the batwings and came toward the bar. Hank's eyes touched briefly and casually on his face and then looked on, but an instant later a shock of recognition coursed through him. He glanced at the man once again, unsure of where he had seen him before, but then it came back to him with blinding clarity.

Stumbling out of the Cougar Saloon, his shirt bloody where Mose Duncan's scattergun had wounded him. . . . Now the third holdup man, the one who had gotten away, was walking right toward Hank.

It couldn't be him, Hank told himself. He had gotten only a glimpse of the man's face that day, and surely he was mistaken now.

But then the man's eyes met Hank's, and recognition flared in them. ''That goddamn kid!'' he exclaimed, and his hand flashed toward his pistol.

Hank knew instinctively that he couldn't outdraw the man. He used the sack of supplies as a makeshift weapon as the outlaw's gun cleared leather. The full sack smacked into the man's hand as the pistol blasted, knocking the barrel aside so that the bullet thumped into the wall. A second later, as the patrons of the saloon scurried for cover, Hank cracked the barrel of the rifle across the man's wrist and sent the handgun spinning away.

The man roared in pain and launched himself forward, grabbing with his left hand for the knife sheathed at his left hip. Hank tried to bring the barrel of the Henry around but was too late. The man crashed into him and both of them went sprawling, Hank falling heavily against one of the tables. Pain shot through his side, but he didn't have time to worry about it. He rolled desperately as the man drove the blade home into the plank floor of the saloon, right where Hank's head had been a second earlier.

The rifle was still in Hank's hand, though he had dropped the sack of supplies when he was knocked down. He swung the weapon around, lashing out with the butt as the man tried to wrench the knife free from the floor. There was a sickening crunch as the metal butt plate caught the man in the jaw. Teeth and blood flew from his mouth as he fell back away from the knife.

Even through the agony of his smashed mouth, he was able to spot the pistol lying on the floor only a few feet from him, where it had fallen when Hank knocked it out of his hand. The man lunged for it, got his fingers on the weapon, and rolled over.

Hank saw the Colt coming up. There was no choice. He fired from the hip. It was almost impossible to miss at this range.

The bullet bored into the man's chest and drove him back down to the floor. The gun slipped out of his fingers. There was just enough time for him to reach for his chest with one hand, a bewildered look on his face, before he died.

Hank was on his knees on the floor about ten feet away, holding the Henry in both hands. Blood was pounding in his head, and as he became aware of a wetness on his side, he looked down and saw that it was staining his shirt, too. Somewhere in the brief scuffle, the bullet wounds had gotten opened up again.

He was surprised that the man had recognized him. During the attempted holdup back in San Saba, Hank had seen him only for a moment, and the same had to be true of the would-be robber. But at a time like that, maybe a man saw things clearer, had them impressed deeper on his brain. Maybe the man had thought that Hank was trailing him.

Suddenly Hank's vision went blurry for a moment. He let go of the rifle with one hand and caught himself as he started to fall forward. The saloon's occupants were starting to poke their heads back out now that the shooting was over. Hank heard a strange, rhythmic thumping sound, and then a strong hand was gripping his arm and helping him to his feet.

"You all right, son?"

Hank looked over and saw a burly young man in his twenties, who was watching him with a look of concern. "I'm fine," Hank said, but he knew he didn't sound too convincing.

The young man gestured at his bloody side. "That fella cut you?"

Hank shook his head and said, "No, that's an old wound." The words made it sound like being wounded was an everyday thing with him, and Hank was aware of the irony and the huge changes in his life.

Another man bulled in through the batwings, moving quickly and holding a pistol in his hand. "What's going on here?" he demanded, his voice gruff.

The man who had helped Hank up stepped forward, and Hank saw the thick wooden peg that took the place of his leg. The man gestured at the corpse on the floor. "That yahoo there made a play, tried to gun down this young fella. We all saw it." He looked around the room challengingly and got several nods of agreement from the bystanders. "The boy didn't have any choice but to shoot him."

The newcomer walked briskly over to Hank. There was

a star pinned to his shirt, just under the edge of his vest. "That the way it happened, boy?" he asked.

Hank nodded. "Yes, sir." His legs were starting to feel like the muscles were melting.

"You have any idea why he threw down on you?"

"Him and two friends of his tried to hold up a saloon in San Saba a few days ago. You look under his shirt and you'll find some buckshot wounds he got then. I helped break it up, stopped the other two from getting away with the money."

The sheriff jerked a thumb at the dead man. "Stopped 'em the same way you did that one, I reckon?"

"Seemed to be the thing to do at the time."

For a long moment, the sheriff regarded him with narrowed eyes, and Hank could tell that he was pondering what to do with him. "All right," the sheriff finally said. "I suppose you're tellin' the truth. And since Tim here says this killin' was self-defense, we'll let it go at that." He holstered his gun and glared at Hank. "But don't you go shootin' up anybody else in my town, understand?"

"I understand, Sheriff," Hank said softly. He blinked rapidly, trying to keep focused on the sheriff, but it wasn't easy.

"Some of you men get that body out of here," the sheriff commanded, turning and leaving.

"You'd better get that looked at," the young man with the wooden leg told Hank as he pointed at the bloodstain on his shirt. "I'll help you over to the barber's."

Hank shook off the hand that the young man placed on his arm. "I'll be all right," he said. "I've been taking care of it."

"But you're hurt—"

"It don't amount to nothing," Hank assured him.

"At least let me get you some salve from over at the store where I work. What've you been using on it?"

Hank smiled. "Chewing tobacco."

The young man made a face. "Whoo-eee! You're lucky

it didn't rot your guts out. Come on." He took Hank's arm again, and this time Hank didn't pull away.

"Name's Tim Reynolds," the young man said as he and Hank walked across the street toward the general store. He held up the sack of supplies that Hank had forgotten about completely. "Looks like you were over here earlier. Must've been right after I left for the day."

"You work in the store regular like?" Hank asked, forcing his brain to concentrate on why he was here in the first place.

"Every damn day," Tim answered. "Since I got back."

"I'm sorry about what happened to you." Hank thought he should say *something*, rather than pretending the man's handicap wasn't there.

Tim shrugged broad shoulders. "I get by," he said. "I was luckier than most."

Hank nodded in understanding as they went up onto the porch. He put his hand out to stop Tim. "I need to ask you a question," he said.

"Sure, go ahead."

"Have you seen some strangers passing through in the last few days? Five men and a couple of women, more than likely traveling in two wagons, maybe three."

Tim considered the question for a moment, then started shaking his head. "Doesn't sound familiar. I waited on a couple of strangers the other day, but they were by themselves." Tim hesitated a moment, then went on, "Of course, they weren't by themselves either, strictly speaking."

"What's that mean?" Hank asked.

"They had their uncle's body with them in a casket in the back of the wagon. Said they were going to bury him over at Bender's Bluff."

He was on the right track. Hank knew that in his guts. And it was only a matter of time until he caught up with the murderers. . . .

"You don't look too good, friend," Tim said worriedly.

I'll go get that salve." Tim went into the store while Hank waited on the sidewalk. He returned a moment later carrying a jar of black ointment that smelled foul when Hank lifted its lid.

"You try some of that," Tim told him. "It'll fix you."

"Th-Thanks," Hank said. He took a handful of coins out of his pocket. "How much?"

"It's on me," Tim assured him. He refused to take any money for the medicine, and Hank didn't have the energy to argue with him. Hank added the jar to his sack of supplies and went to his horse to tie it onto the saddle.

Tim stared at him. "You're not riding out tonight?"

"I'll put a few more miles behind me," Hank said as he pulled himself up into the saddle and rested the Henry across the pommel.

"I thought sure you'd stay the night."

"I'll make camp up the trail a ways."

Tim stepped closer to the horse and held up his hand. "I never got your name."

Hank took his hand and returned the firm grip. "Hank Littleton. I'm pleased to meet you, Mr. Reynolds. Thank you for all your help."

"No trouble." Tim released Hank's hand and stepped back. "You be careful now, Hank."

Hank nodded and reined the horse around, heeling it into motion. "Be seein' you," he called over his shoulder.

Tim Reynolds doubted that as he watched Hank ride off down the street. He had an unpleasant feeling that the boy wouldn't be coming back this way. He was a close-mouthed one, that Hank Littleton was, but it was obvious he was on some kind of mission, some quest that he considered noble.

And folks like that mostly wound up dead.

Ten

A man's mind might be obsessed, but his body still had to rest every now and then. Thaddeus Kimbell was no exception. No matter how badly he wanted to close in on Clayborne and his gang, he knew he had to stop occasionally for a full night's sleep.

Now, as he lay wrapped in his blankets in a little grassy clearing, he slept fitfully, thrashing from side to side every few minutes. The night was hot, and Kimbell was dreaming.

He was with Louise again in his dream, Louise of the pale, pale skin that was sometimes cool and sometimes so damned hot to his touch. . . . There had never been much time for women in his life. The army had been his mistress. But he was lost as soon as he saw Louise at the sutler's store there in Fort Smith. She had smiled at him, and the smile was full of such promise that he had been drawn inexorably to her. He had to know if the delights hinted at in her eyes could ever possibly be his.

He had learned. The nights had been long, but never long enough. Always, Kimbell was left wanting more. He knew that Louise was traveling with a man named Abner

Clayborne, a southern planter and supporter of the Confederacy. Kimbell tried not to have any illusions, tried to be a realist and a pragmatist, but when he was with Louise, he dared to believe that she meant what she was saying to him, believed that she would stay with him and let Clayborne and his party go on to wherever they were going.

It had all been lies, of course. All she had really wanted from him was the information about when the gold shipment would be arriving and how it would be guarded.

Kimbell moaned, his sleep haunted by a dark-eyed ghost who caressed him with soft fingers, with warm lips and tongue. His hands ripped the blankets from around him, and then his fingers clenched and unclenched into fists. He hated her so much, and needed her so badly. He shook suddenly, jerked upright, and let out a little cry. His eyes darted around wildly for a moment before he realized where he was.

He stretched back out and closed his eyes. His thoughts kept going back to his last night with Louise. He had known that he shouldn't be with her, that duty demanded he be on hand when the gold arrived at the fort. The time of its arrival was a secret. He knew, and General Nathan knew, but they were the only ones on the post with that knowledge. The men in the guard detail had no idea what was in the wagon they were accompanying.

Therefore, they weren't expecting the sudden attack that had come while the wagon was still over two miles away from the fort. The shots had come from ambush, ripping into the troopers and blowing them out of their saddles. One noncom had survived somehow, despite the four wounds in his body, to come crawling into the fort hours later and tell the story. Kimbell didn't know for sure, but he felt certain that the bushwhackers had been those two who worked for Clayborne. Guides, that was what they were supposed to be. Hired guns was more like it. And that slimy Reuben Reed, he had probably been in on it as well.

Clayborne hadn't dirtied his hands with any of the actual killing, though. Kimbell knew that for a fact. Because Clayborne had come to Louise's hotel room that night, had held a gun on him while Louise dressed. When Kimbell realized what they had done, he would have charged, regardless of the weapon, had his muscles obeyed his commands. But it was too late. The drug that Louise had slipped into his drinks was already dragging him down, even as she laughed at him. Though he fought it with every ounce of determination he possessed, he felt himself slipping into sleep, a sleep from which he would never awaken.

At least, that was what Clayborne had told him. The man had enjoyed gloating over his helpless foe. Victim, that was a better word. To be someone's foe, you at least had to put up a fight, and he had been putty in Louise's hands. They had gotten what they wanted from him without a struggle.

He had crossed them up, though. He hadn't died. When they were gone, he managed somehow to get out of bed, had stayed awake long enough to stagger to the landing and go toppling naked down the stairs into the hotel lobby. The fall bruised and battered him, to say nothing of the disgrace and scandal it caused. But it had kept him from slipping down that dark well with no bottom. . . .

The army had been his whole life, but now, for the first time, he had something else to live for. Thoughts of revenge filled his head through the long days in the stockade. After he escaped, he was not going to let Louise and Clayborne enjoy the fruits of their treachery.

The two wagons rolled along, the Conestoga still in the lead. Behind them, Thomas Littleton's corpse lay sprawled in a gully. Clayborne had decided that the body had served its purpose, so they dumped it much as they had Hank's.

The sky overhead was clear for the moment as night fell, but before the next day was over, the buzzards would arrive, drawn by their instincts, and would circle overhead for a while in a grim memorial to death.

In the back of the Conestoga, Beth Shelby stared out the way they had come. The shadows were closing in on her, and not all of them came from the advent of night. Her eyes were glazed, and she had the look of someone caught in an awful dream.

But this was no dream. There would be no waking up to safety. This was all terribly, horribly real. . . .

Night came and brought with it a touch of coolness, but the air was still stifling. Louise thought that she would never be cool again. She had lived with heat and sweat for so long now that she had to concentrate on the future just to keep going. Clayborne had never been to Mexico, but he had talked to people who had, and he was full of stories about snow-topped mountains and crisp clean air and pastures of tall green grass. Just thinking about it made Louise feel a little more comfortable. Not much, but a little was better than nothing.

Clayborne moved up behind her and rested his hands on her shoulders. "Feeling better?" he asked.

"I suppose. How far are we from Mexico?"

Clayborne considered. "I think another two weeks should see us there, if we don't run into any trouble."

"Two weeks," Louise sighed. "I didn't know it could sound so long."

Clayborne leaned over and kissed the back of her neck. His hands worked on her shoulders. "It will be worth all the time and effort, darling. You'll see."

"I hope so," Louise whispered. After all this time, though, she didn't really believe it. Still, she let him cup her chin in his hand and twist her head around. His lips came down hard and demanding on hers, and she knew that he would want to visit her in the wagon tonight. She had given up trying to make excuses to get Beth out of the way. Now she just told her sister to go sit by the fire for a while. Beth understood, even if she didn't like it.

"No! Get away from her!"

Clayborne and Louise jerked their heads apart and looked up to see Beth standing there. Her face was contorted, and she was quivering all over with emotion.

There was a gun in her hand.

Louise caught her breath as she recognized the little nickel-plated .25 revolver. It was hers, and she usually kept it in one of her trunks. Beth knew about it, and knew that the bullets were kept with the gun. There was every chance that it was loaded.

Beth pointed the pistol at Clayborne and repeated, "Get away from my sister, you murderer!"

"It's all right, Beth," Louise said, trying to keep her voice calm and quiet. "Abner's not going to hurt me."

"He's a murderer! I've got to save you. He'll hurt you, I know he will. He always hurts people."

Ignacio Jiménez wandered into the clearing, finished with his work. The horses were bedded down for the night. He stopped short when he heard Beth's strident tones and saw the gun in her hand. His eyes widened.

Reed was ready to make his move. Clayborne took a deep breath and nodded to him. Beth realized too late that someone was behind her, and she tried to twist around.

Reed lunged forward, savagely wrenching the weapon out of Beth's fingers. She let out a little cry, and then Reed brought his other hand around. The palm lashed across her face in a ringing slap.

"No!" Louise shouted, running toward the struggling couple. "Get your hands off her, you bastard!"

Clayborne caught Louise's arm and jerked her to a stop. He shoved her roughly behind him as she strode forward. Beth had raised a hand to her face and stood holding her bruised cheek. She looked like an animal petrified with fear as she watched Clayborne approach her.

"You pointed a gun at me," Clayborne said in a low, intense voice. "I won't stand for that, Beth. I simply won't stand for it."

His hand flashed up. Beth didn't even try to dodge as he drove his fist into her face. She staggered a couple of steps, went down on a knee.

Louise grabbed Clayborne from behind and tried to hold him back. "Damn you, Abner!" she cried. "Leave her alone!"

Clayborne shook his head. His eyes were icy as he said, "She has to learn her lesson." He reached to his waist and unbuckled his belt, pulling the broad leather strap free.

Louise saw what he intended and began beating futilely on his back. Clayborne reached behind him and shoved her away again. "Keep her off me, Reuben," he ordered.

Reed moved more quickly than Louise expected, grabbing her and lifting her so that her feet dangled inches off the ground. She writhed and twisted in his grip, but he was too strong. She couldn't free herself. Reed carried her off to the side several yards as Clayborne came closer to Beth, the belt dangling loosely from his hands.

"You have to take your punishment," he told the young girl. "And you can never be disrespectful of me again. Do you understand? If you do, maybe you can still come with us. Otherwise, I'll leave you out here."

"Nooo!" Louise wailed, but Reed just held her tighter.

Beth's lip curled. She spat on Clayborne's boot.

His face rippled with emotion as he lifted the belt and brought it down around Beth's shoulders. She screamed and tried to dodge, but the belt rose and fell, rose and fell, until all she could do was whimper in pain and jerk spasmodically as the strap lashed her body.

Louise closed her eyes. She couldn't bear to watch her sister being beaten.

Clayborne lifted the belt for another stroke, but as his

hand started downward, strong brown fingers suddenly locked around his wrist and stopped it short. He looked over, astounded that anyone would defy him, and met the dark gaze of Ignacio Jiménez.

"Leave her alone, *señor*," Jiménez grated. "Do not touch her again."

Slowly, a smile spread over Clayborne's lips. "Why, Ignacio," he said, "what a surprising display of spirit." He opened his fingers and let the belt fall to the ground. "I didn't think you had it in you."

Jiménez released Clayborne's wrist and stepped back, looking as if he had surprised himself just as much as he had the others. "I'm sorry. . . ." he started to say.

Clayborne reached under his coat and brought out a small pistol of his own. "It won't happen again," he said.

The gun went off with a sharp crack. Jiménez took a step backward and reached up to his chest. He shook his head. Then, as the stain underneath his fingers grew, he slipped down onto his knees and then slowly fell forward.

Clayborne turned away from him, already dismissing him from his mind. He gestured to Reed. "You can let her go now, Reuben," he said. "Louise won't cause any trouble."

As soon as Louise's feet touched the ground, she ran forward and dropped to her knees beside Beth, who was huddled, sobbing. The back of Beth's dress was blood-stained. Louise reached out tentatively and touched her younger sister's hair. Her lips formed the words *I'm sorry*, but no sound came out.

Clayborne jerked his head at Jiménez and said to Reed, "Make sure he's dead." Reed hurried forward and rolled the Mexican over onto his back. Jiménez's face was frozen in a surprised expression.

"He's dead, all right," Reed said a moment later.

Running footsteps sounded, and a second later, Ordway and Smith burst into the camp. "What happened?" Ordway demanded.

"Our little party has been reduced by one member,"

Clayborne said casually. "Ignacio decided he could no longer accompany us."

Louise helped Beth to her feet, letting the girl lean heavily on her. Awkwardly, they started toward the Conestoga. As they passed Clayborne, Louise paused and hissed, "You'll pay for this, Abner."

The expression Clayborne gave her was smug. "I don't think so, my dear. You're outraged right now, but your greed will win out in the end. You won't do anything to upset your own little schemes."

Louise shook her head. "You're wrong." Her voice was utterly sincere as she went on, "I'm going to kill you, you son of a bitch. Someday I'm going to kill you."

Standing beside Jiménez's body, Reed shook his head without thinking. That was the wrong thing to tell Clayborne, the wrong attitude to take with him right now. Reed had seen the insanity in Clayborne's eyes as he whipped Beth Shelby.

He had enjoyed it.

Clayborne took a deep breath. "If that's the way you feel about it, you leave me no choice, Louise. But I will miss you."

"What are you talking about?" Louise asked.

"I'm not a fool, Louise," Clayborne told her. "And I'd have to be a fool to take you with me after you've promised to kill me, now wouldn't I?"

"You mean it," Louise whispered. Beth was still trembling in her arms. "You'd actually leave us out here."

"That's exactly what I'm going to do." Clayborne turned away from her and waved a hand at Reed, Ordway, and Smith. "Get loaded up," he told them. "We're pulling out. I don't like traveling at night, but I'm not going to stay here. We'll find another camp farther on down the trail."

"You can't do it, Abner," Louise said. Her arm tightened around Beth's shoulders.

"I can and will." Clayborne spoke to Ordway and Smith again. "I told you to get ready to move out."

Ordway and Smith both nodded somewhat reluctantly. They were hard men, but the idea of abandoning two women out here like this grated on them.

Still, Clayborne had the gold. For the time being, his word was law.

"Let's get at it," Ordway said flatly.

Louise and Beth watched as the wagons rolled out of the clearing, followed by Ordway, Smith, and the little remuda. Beth was crying again, and Louise felt curiously empty inside. She knew she should run screaming after Clayborne, should plead with him and throw herself on his mercy—

Except that he didn't have any mercy. He was dead inside, and Louise knew that now. There was nothing she could do. Nothing. . . .

For a while they could hear the creak of wheels, the jangle of harness, the steady plodding of the horses.

But when that was gone, silence fell over the plains.

Eleven

Hank knew he was in trouble. The wounds in his side burned all the time now, and the flesh around them hurt. The salve that Tim Reynolds had given him had seemed to help at first, but now it didn't do a thing. Neither did the chewing-tobacco poultices when he went back to them. Hank knew he had to have help if he was going to survive.

But where, in God's name, was he going to find help in this trackless wilderness?

Bender's Bluff had been a wild-goose chase, but even the fever wasn't going to throw Hank off the trail. He continued heading west, swaying in the saddle.

It was early evening now, and the lowering sun glared against his eyes. He was developing a permanent squint, he supposed. His head throbbed, but that went on all the time now. He was getting used to it. The pain in his side was also a dull ache, with an occasional twinge like fire. Something about the way the horizon was tilted didn't seem quite right to him, but he couldn't figure why.

Maybe he was delirious. Maybe that was why he heard singing and then the boom of gunshots.

Hank reined in and frowned. He could have sworn the sounds were real and not the phantoms of a feverish brain.

There was only one gun firing, to judge by the brief delay between shots. Reloading would explain that. Hank urged his horse slowly forward, trying to get it straight in his mind where the sounds were coming from.

The country around here was flat for the most part, but there were stretches where it could get pretty rough. He was just entering one of those areas. Gullies unexpectedly cut through the land, wandering crazily across the plains. There wasn't much grass anymore, and what there was had begun to dry up. Mesquites choked the bottom of the draws.

The shooting and singing seemed to come from up ahead. Hank narrowed his eyes and reined in as he spotted movement. A figure flitted from one bush to another, and Hank got a split-second impression of dark, bare skin. A moment later, a similar figure darted into sight and then back out.

Indians. Hank shook his head in an effort to clear it. The Indians must not have seen him yet, or they would be firing at him. He swung down hurriedly, catching the saddlehorn for a moment as his balance threatened to desert him. The Henry rifle slid smoothly out of its boot, and he held it in one hand while he led the horse into the scant concealment of a patch of brush. He tied the reins, then checked the loads in the Remington on his hip.

He didn't know how many Indians were out there, but he felt fairly certain there were more than the two he had seen. He had heard enough old-timers talk to know that they seldom traveled in bands smaller than three or four. These were Apaches, more than likely, maybe Lipans.

The Sharps blasted again as Hank slipped forward. He could understand some of the words of the song now, and it was bawdy enough to border on being obscene. The singer sounded like he was having a damned good time, too.

There was a crackle of fire from smaller caliber weapons, and the Apaches were flickering shadows as they charged forward through the brush. Hank could tell now that they were heading for a little ridge beside one of the gullies. They had someone cornered there. As Hank heard the Sharps once again, he saw the smoke thinly drift against the sky.

From the sound of his voice, the singer was a white man. Hank didn't know who would be insane enough to sing in the face of an Indian attack, but he knew that he had to help the man. He came out of his crouch and brought the rifle to his shoulder, fighting to ignore the pain he felt in his head and side as he aimed. The Indians were charging out in the open now, a good half dozen of them leaving the cover of the brush and running toward the ridge. They had pistols and carbines looted from white men's ranches, and they poured a storm of lead at their quarry.

Hank lined his sights on one of the running braves and squeezed the trigger.

The Henry bucked against his shoulder. He thought he saw his target stumble and grab at a wounded leg, but by then Hank was shifting his sights and firing again. He worked the lever on the rifle quickly between each shot as he emptied the chamber.

Two of the Indians were down, and the others were whirling around to see where this new threat was coming from. That proved to be a mistake.

A figure came over the top of the ridge, singing at the top of its lungs. Hank blinked, unable to see clearly against the glare of the setting sun. The man was big, he could tell that much. And he had a weapon in each hand. He lifted the Sharps and fired it one-handed, the heavy ball smashing the spine of one of the Apaches. The man's handgun boomed almost as loudly as the rifle, and another Indian went spinning to the dirt. Then he was among the other two, dropping the big rifle and yanking a knife from his belt. He slashed from side to side—

Hank's vision blurred. He staggered as the blood pounded in his head. He was going to die, and Clayborne would get away, and his grandfather's death would go unavenged.

The Henry slipped from his fingers, as it abruptly became too heavy to hold. He felt himself falling and put his hands out. They jarred against the sandy ground. Screams pierced the air, then a silence dropped down. Hank closed his eyes and tried to get his breath.

He heard footsteps coming toward him. He pushed himself up and rolled over onto his back, looking up at the sky. It was starting to darken in the east, but the west was still gloriously bright with the setting sun.

A shadow loomed over him.

God, the man was big! Not just tall, but wide as well. He seemed to blot out the whole sky. He was hatless, and his dark bushy hair was tangled. His full beard was the same shade but with streaks of gray. Silhouetted as he was, Hank couldn't make out the man's features. A strong, piercing smell came from him, though, and it became even more pungent as the man leaned closer to him.

"Yuh hurt, boy?" It was the same booming voice that had been singing earlier, singing in the face of death. "Don't you worry none. Them Injuns are dead, and ol' Buffalo will take right good care of you."

Arms that seemed like tree trunks went around Hank, and he felt himself being lifted. That smell washed over him again, and he started to gag. His side hurt like hell.

He gave it up and closed his eyes. Maybe he would live and maybe he wouldn't, but there wasn't one more damn thing he could do about the matter.

There was warmth on the right side of his face. Hank heard a crackling noise and slowly realized that he was lying beside a campfire. He tried to draw a deep breath and couldn't. There was something tight around his middle.

EPITAPH

The big bearded man had taken care of him, just like he had promised. Hank felt a surge of pure relief at the simple fact that he wasn't dead.

He opened his eyes, blinking them against the light cast by the fire. Sensing movement near him, he rolled his head to the side and looked the other way.

The ugliest animal he had ever seen hissed at him and drew back.

Hank jerked back instinctively. The varmint was small, but it had a long scarred snout and rows of sharp teeth. Coarse gray fur bristled over its body except on the long naked tail that it exhibited as it turned and waddled away.

He had never known that a possum could be so damned ugly, or smell so bad. That reminded him of his rescuer, and he started to look around the camp for him.

"See you met ol' Stink." The voice came from the edge of the circle of light. The big man stepped closer and bent over to catch the possum's tail. He lifted the animal up, grinning as it flailed its stubby legs and hissed again.

Hank licked his dry lips and croaked, "I don't think he likes my looks."

"Don't like your scent, more likely. Possum can't see a damned thing less'n it's right on top of its snout. Blindest critters you'll ever see this side of a bat." He reached out and rubbed blunt fingers against the animal's belly. "Don't know why I like the little bastard."

Hank tried to raise his head but had to let it fall back. A little groan escaped from his lips, even though he tried to hold it in.

The big man put the possum back on the ground and came over to Hank. He knelt down and said, "You just rest easy, younker. Won't nothing else happen to you here."

Hank stared up at him, thinking that he was the strangest-looking fellow he had ever seen. His darkly tanned face was creased and weathered, and an ugly white scar cut across it right beside the left eye. Another fraction of an inch during the altercation that had produced the scar and he would have been blinded in that eye for sure. His long hair was twisted into a braid just in front of the left ear, and something was attached to that braid. Hank had to look twice before he realized the object was the rattle from a rattlesnake. There were at least fifteen bands on the rattle, which meant that its original owner must have been one hell of a snake.

The man had a filthy blanket poncho over his shoulders, and some of the distinctive smell was coming from it. It was decorated with a row of drawings that looked as if they had been done by an Indian. Hank saw buffalos and tepees painted on the fabric, and there was some fancy beadwork to set them off. At one time, the poncho must have been a beautiful garment, but it had seen a lot of dirt and sweat.

"Name's Buffalo Newcomb," he went on in his rumbling voice as he knelt beside Hank. He pulled a pipe with a long, curved stem from under the poncho and started to fill it from a greasy leather pouch.

"Hank . . . Hank Littleton."

"Well, I'm right pleased to meet yuh, Hank Littleton. Reckon you saved this pilgrim's worthless hide back yonder when you lit into them 'Paches. They'da had my hair in another few minutes."

"You . . . saved me," Hank said.

Buffalo Newcomb took a twig from the fire and held it to the pipe, puffing until he had it lit. The smoke was surprisingly fragrant, Hank thought.

"Hell, I just doctored you up a mite." Buffalo frowned. "Where'n hell'd a younker like you get shot up like that?"

Hank was too tired to go into the story. He said instead, "Some men made a mistake."

His voice must have been grim, because Buffalo blew out a cloud of smoke and grinned. "And now you're after 'em, right? Ridin' the vengeance trail?" His tone was mocking.

Hank grimaced and didn't make any reply. It was hard for people to understand, he supposed. He wasn't doing this because he wanted to, but because he had to.

"Hell, don't fret over it, son," Buffalo went on. "Reckon you can tell me all about it later. Right now you could do with some more sleep. Give them holes in your side a chance to heal up."

"They're festering," Hank said, his voice weak.

"Hell, I know that. Why do you think I used my special remedy on 'em? Ain't nothin' better for a gunshot wound than ol' Buffalo's special possum-piss poultice, boy."

Hank closed his eyes.

Hank's sleep was restless that night, but every time he awoke, Buffalo Newcomb was there to give him a drink of water or just to speak reassuringly in that thunderous voice. By midmorning of the next day, Hank felt better. His head was clearer, and with Buffalo's help, he sat up.

The fever seemed to be gone, and when it left, Hank's appetite came back. He eagerly ate the meat and bread that Buffalo offered him and followed it with several cups of hot coffee. Once the food was in him, he started to feel downright human again.

Buffalo had brought his horse into camp and tied it near a rangy old mule. There was a packhorse, too, but evidently the ugly, long-eared animal was the one Buffalo used for riding. It seemed to fit his personality. The little possum called Stink stayed around the camp, at times following its master around like a puppy.

Hank cast a dubious glance at the possum and said to Buffalo, "You were funning me about that poultice, right?"

"Was I?" Buffalo asked.

"You used a plant or an herb or something to pack the wounds, didn't you?"

"Well, I reckon I could have. Don't you go thinkin' that possum piss ain't good medicine, though."

Hank didn't know what to believe, but he felt better,

and that was all that was really important. He waited until Buffalo sat down cross-legged beside the ashes of the fire and then asked, "What were you doing out here by yourself?"

"Runnin' from them heathens, mostly. They come up on me yesterday about noon, and I led 'em a merry chase, let me tell you. Probably still be runnin' from 'em if the damned mule hadn't up and stopped. I got the animals down in that draw and forted up on the ridge, but there was too many Apaches. One of 'em would've got me sooner or later."

He had Hank's rifle cradled in his massive hands and was turning it over carefully, examining the weapon as he talked.

"Fine piece o' work," he went on, looking up. "Don't reckon it's got the stoppin' power of my Sharps, but havin' more'n one shot must come in handy."

"It can," Hank said.

"You don't talk a whole hell of a lot, do you? Me, I talk all the damn time. Drives Stink and the mule crazy. Sing a lot, too. Write a song about ever'body I meet. Suppose I'll have to write one about you now, since it looks like I ain't goin' to have to bury you."

"I heard you singing during the fight," Hank said. "You sounded like you were enjoying it."

Buffalo shrugged his wide shoulders. "Might as well enjoy whatever comes to you, I say. I might've wound up dead if you hadn't come along, but it would've been a hell of a fight." He grinned, revealing large brown teeth. " 'Sides, it throws them redskins off. They sometimes sing when they're goin' into battle, but they ain't used to somebody warblin' back at 'em."

He stood up and replaced the Henry rifle in its saddle boot. As the poncho lifted and swung back, Hank saw the big Dragoon Colt in a holster on Buffalo's hip, and sheathed behind it was an Arkansas Toothpick.

"What are you going to do now?" Hank asked.

Buffalo looked down at him and frowned. "Why, I

reckon I'll wait for you to heal up, son. You can't travel like that. Ridin' all the time and not takin' care of yourself is what got you into such a fix."

"You . . . want us to ride together?"

Buffalo looked at him for a long moment, his grizzled face twisted in thought. Finally he said, "I'm just driftin', Hank. No place special. Now, you ain't told me just who you're after or why, but I reckon you might could use some company."

Hank nodded slowly. "Thank you," he said.

"Don't thank me, boy." The smile on his face became savage. "I'm kind of hankerin' to see you use that there fine rifle again."

That night, Hank told him about what had happened in San Saba. As he talked, the memories came back so strongly and vividly that he had a hard time keeping a catch out of his voice. Buffalo snorted in derision when he got to the yarn that Reed had spun about being a Confederate agent.

"Your grandpa must've been an honest man to believe a story like that," he said.

"He was honest," Hank said stiffly.

"Reckon they counted on that. Sometimes a feller who's honest is the easiest one to get took."

Hank went on with the story, and Buffalo frowned and shook his head when he heard how Thomas had been killed and Hank had been left for dead.

"It'd take a pure-dee skunk to do such a thing," he declared. "Why'n hell did they start shootin'?"

"Gold," Hank said simply. "That's why they wanted the special coffin. I think they were really carrying a lot of gold and wanted a place to hide it."

"You don't know that, though," Buffalo said sharply.

Hank shook his head. "No, I don't. And I don't care. Why they did it doesn't matter. All that matters is finding them."

"I reckon that's true," Buffalo nodded solemnly. "I

reckon it makes sense, though. Anybody totin' that much would want a good place to squirrel it away.''

"Maybe I'll ask Clayborne . . . before I kill him.''

Buffalo stared off into the shadows for a long moment, then glanced back at Hank. "You sure you want to do that?''

"I'm sure.''

"Killin' a man ain't always easy. . . .''

"I've killed men before,'' Hank said, his voice flat. "It was necessary then. It's necessary now.''

"Reckon maybe that's right. You've got a long time in front of you, though, and you've got to take whatever you do along with you ever' damn step of the way.''

Hank didn't say anything. Finally, Buffalo nodded and stood up. "Reckon you know what you're doin','' he said. "We'll move on in a day or two.''

"You're still going along?'' Hank asked.

"Said I was, didn't I?'' Buffalo grinned that big grin. "Hell, it's been quite a spell since me and Stink seen us a town. We'll have us a right smart time, won't we, Stink?'' He picked up a mesquite limb and thrust it at the possum, who grabbed it in his sharp teeth and bit through it with a growl. "Feisty little bastard, ain't he?'' Buffalo asked proudly.

Hank closed his eyes and leaned back. Traveling with Buffalo Newcomb was going to be an experience.

Twelve

The next two days passed slowly for Hank. He wanted to be moving on, and the knowledge that he was getting farther and farther behind Clayborne rankled him. Buffalo was right, though; he needed some time to recover.

"Once we get started, we can push along at a right good clip," Buffalo promised. "Ought to catch up to them 'bout the time they hit El Paso."

On the afternoon of the second day, Hank felt good enough to practice his draw with the Remington. He didn't fire the pistol, since he didn't want to draw Indians to them, but he worked on drawing it rapidly and smoothly.

After watching, Buffalo spoke up. "You ain't been usin' a handgun very long, have you, boy?"

Hank grimaced. "Is it that obvious?" He gestured at the Henry leaning against a nearby rock and went on, "I guess I'm just more at home with a rifle."

"Reckon it all depends on what you're shootin' at." Buffalo patted the butt of the Dragoon Colt. "This here hogleg ain't too accurate, but it'll sure knock a man down, happen you can hit him. The Sharps is better for long-range work. And for close-in chores . . ." He grinned and slipped his knife from its sheath. "Can't beat this ol' Arkansas Toothpick."

Hank had a vague recollection of Buffalo wading into the Apaches with the broad-bladed knife. His memory of that whole incident was sort of blurry, just like his vision had been at the time. But evidently Buffalo had done all right with the knife. He was still alive, and the Indians weren't.

Reholstering the Remington, Hank said, "I'm feeling a lot stronger this afternoon. You think we could move on?"

"It'd be a good idea, in the mornin'," Buffalo nodded. "Them braves we kilt the other day probably weren't missed for a while, seein' as they was most likely a wanderin' war party, but they got folks somewhere. Sooner or later, somebody's goin' to come lookin' for them, and I'd just as soon light a shuck 'fore then."

"How long will it take to get to El Paso?"

Buffalo shrugged. "Depends on what trouble we run into. Don't worry, son, we'll get there in time."

"And if we don't?"

"Well, hell, there's always Mexico. Ain't been there in a while." Buffalo's grin took on a lecherous tilt. "There's some pretty señoritas down there I wouldn't mind gettin' reacquainted with, if you get my drift."

Hank did, but he didn't know what to say in reply, so he turned and started practicing with the Remington again. The effort of the draw made his side twinge slightly, but now that the fever was gone he didn't mind a little pain.

Mention of Mexico had gotten Buffalo Newcomb in a reminiscing mood. He reached up and fingered the scar on his face. "Got this down south of the border," he said, then paused, obviously waiting for some reaction from Hank.

Well, the man had saved his life. "How did it happen?"

"Got into a ruckus over one o' them señoritas, just like

you'd figure. She thought a big gringo like me was just about the handsomest thing she'd ever seen. She was singin' in a cantina, and there was a bunch of folks there, but it seemed like she was singin' just to me. Leastways, I felt that way, and come to find out, she did, too. We got together later, had us a high ol' time. But then this other feller showed up. Turns out he was sweet on her hisself, and he was some high and mighty *bandido* who had a gang thereabouts. He started in hoorawin' me and tellin' me he was goin' to kill me for touchin' his girlfriend. To hear him tell it, she was innocent as a newborn calf till I come along. Well, *that* was a damned lie, I'm here to tell you. That gal weren't innocent. Don't care what she'd told him."

Hank grinned, caught up in the story. He squatted in the shade and listened to Buffalo's rumbling voice.

"So when he busts in like that and starts makin' them threats, well, naturally I get my own back up a mite. Ask him what army's goin' to do all this killin' he's yellin' about. Well, that was a mistake, 'cause he calls in that gang of his and all of 'em commence to jumpin' on me. The gal is screamin' and all them Mexes are cussin' me out and I tend to make a little noise myself when I go to fightin', so we raised a hell of a commotion for a while before things settled down."

"Before things settled down?" Hank echoed. "What happened? How did you get out of a mess like that?"

"Mexes like to fight with a knife. A blade's almost like a woman to 'em and you'd do well to recollect that. So I got cut up some 'fore they decided their honor weren't so offended after all. Plus I unlimbered my Dragoon and blasted holes in a few of 'em. Pity about the gal."

"What happened to her?"

"Got in the way of the muzzle once when I was burnin' powder at her greaser friends." Buffalo's tone was sorrowful. "Sure did mess 'er up, but it was a pure-dee accident. I reckon she brought it on her own self. Found out later she was just tryin' to make her feller jealous.

She succeeded, all right, but it didn't do neither of 'em any good, them bein' dead and all.''

Hank looked down at the ground. He wasn't sure that the señorita's death had been as accidental as Buffalo claimed it was, but he wasn't going to admit that doubt, least of all to Buffalo himself. Finally, he said noncommittally, ''Sounds like you've had an interesting life.''

''That I have, boy. Remind me to tell you about it sometime.''

Hank smiled. Buffalo hadn't been doing much *except* talking for the last two days, spinning yarn after yarn about his exciting adventures. About half the time, Hank didn't believe a word he was saying, but he had to admit that Buffalo could have been telling the truth about all of it. Out here, the most unlikely things could happen.

His side was still bandaged, but Hank felt like he would soon be able to move again without any stiffness plaguing him. The head wound was almost completely healed.

''I'd like to pull out first thing in the morning,'' he told Buffalo.

''Fine by me.'' Buffalo leaned over and plucked the possum from the ground, lifting it by its tail. He idly scratched the animal's back, watching as it squirmed and tried to turn around so that it could bite. ''Me 'n' Stink'll be glad to get back on the trail. Stink don't like to stay in one place too long.''

Hank had gotten that impression about Buffalo, too.

That night Hank checked his gear and made sure everything would be ready to go the next morning. His supplies were holding out well, and if he and Buffalo rode together to El Paso, they might have enough between them to make any more stops unnecessary.

As night fell, Hank rolled up in his blankets and tried to sleep. It would be chilly by morning, even during the summer. Buffalo bedded down on the other side of the fire, which was out now. The little possum was wandering around, as it usually did at night, and Hank hoped it wouldn't come across a coyote with an empty belly.

Personally, he thought Stink was about the ugliest, meanest, smelliest animal he'd ever seen, but Buffalo seemed to be attached to the varmint.

Sleep didn't come easy. Hank was too keyed up about getting back on the trail the next day, he supposed. He stared up at the stars, floating randomly in the night sky, and thought that his own life had become like that these last few days. He had thought that there were patterns in his life just like there were supposed to be pictures in the stars. But he had always thought that people who saw archers and crabs and things like that in the stars had better imagination than eyesight. That was the way it had been with him ever since that attempted robbery back in San Saba. It took a big stretch of the imagination to make sense of what had happened since then.

His eyes closed, and he drifted off to sleep without being aware of it. For a while the camp was dark and quiet, the only sound being the snores emanating from the bulky shadow marking Buffalo Newcomb's position.

Hank was restless, and his thoughts about the holdup must have stirred his memories, because in his dreams he began reliving that day. There were differences this time. The men he had shot fell from their horses all right, but then they got back up, their shirts bloody, and started dancing some crazy jig like they were puppets. Hank shot them again. He could see the bullets smacking into their bodies, crushing flesh and making blood spurt into the air, but still they didn't fall. Instead, they started shooting, and the townspeople began to fall, all of Hank's friends and acquaintances dying in front of his eyes.

Hank rolled over in his sleep and let out a low moan. The two gunmen had been joined now by the third one, the one Hank hadn't killed until San Angelo. He was doing the same dance, killing the same people over and over again.

Somehow the Apaches he had killed while helping Buffalo had appeared in San Saba, too, and though Hank shot them, they wouldn't die. One of them grabbed Rose

Ellen Hobbs off the sidewalk and slit her throat before scalping her. One of the robbers blew Jimmy Maxwell's brains out.

And no matter how many times Hank shot them, no matter how loudly he cried or how bitterly he cursed, there wasn't one damn thing he could do to stop them. The streets of San Saba were running with blood when the dead men finally turned toward Hank and started advancing on him. . . .

He screamed.

He came upright off his blankets, his mouth wide open and cries ripping from his throat. Strong hands seized his arms and shook him, but he twisted and tried to throw them off. He found the strength somewhere to tear free of their grip.

Rolling across the sandy ground, Hank came up onto his feet and plunged off into the darkness. He was overcome with terror and just wanted to get away.

Buffalo caught him about twenty yards from the ashes of the fire, grabbing him and lifting him up so that his feet were off the ground. Hank screamed again and tried to fight. Buffalo grunted a curse. He couldn't get too rough, otherwise he might bust Hank's wounds open again.

"Dammit, Hank, hush up!" Buffalo commanded. "It's me, Buffalo. You're all right, you hear me? You're all right! Ain't nobody goin' to hurt you."

Slowly, Hank's struggles subsided. He shook his head to clear it and then looked down into Buffalo's bearded, grotesque face, recognizing it in the moonlight. After a moment, when his breath came back to him and his heart quit trying to jump out of his chest, he said, "I . . . I'm all right now, Buffalo. You can put me down."

"You ain't goin' to start howlin' again?"

Hank shook his head.

Buffalo lowered him to the ground and let him go. He stepped back and took a deep breath. "Hell, boy, you was yellin' fit to wake the dead. Or ever' Apache in ten miles, and that's worse."

"Wake the dead. . . ." Hank whispered, the dream coming back to him. He sank down cross-legged on the ground and put his head in his hands. He wasn't crying, but his shoulders shook with the intensity of his feelings.

Buffalo put a hand on his shoulder. "What is it, boy?" he asked, trying to tone down the booming of his voice. "You thinkin' about your grandpa?"

Without looking up, Hank shook his head again. "Thinking about all the men I've killed," he said softly. "Two weeks ago I'd never even killed an animal except for food, and now I've killed five men."

"Hell, you didn't have any choice."

"Maybe not. But the last three of them didn't even bother me." Now he lifted his head and raised his gaze to Buffalo. "What am I turning into? The same sort of man as Clayborne, who kills anyone who gets in his way?"

Buffalo shifted his feet uncomfortably. "Damned if I know what any of us are turnin' into," he said after a moment. "But from what you told me 'bout him, I don't reckon that Clayborne feller ever has nightmares. Seems to me that's a mighty important difference right there."

"Maybe so."

"I do know one thing," Buffalo said. "When a man's tryin' to kill me, I reckon I'd be a damn fool not to try to get him first."

Hank couldn't argue with that. He nodded after a moment and said, "I suppose you're right."

"Damned right I am." Buffalo held out a hand and helped Hank to his feet. "Let's get on back to camp. Reckon we'd better both get some more sleep 'fore mornin'."

Hank didn't care at the moment if he ever slept again, and he knew it would be a long time before he dozed off again. The dream had just been too vivid to ease its hold on him quickly.

But Buffalo was right. Morning was going to come

early, and then they'd be on the trail. On the trail of the men that Hank still intended to kill. . . .

Louise Shelby was sure now that she and Beth were going to die. They had been out here in this wilderness for a day and a night now, and it was hard to decide what was going to kill them first—heat, thirst, starvation, snakes, or some wild animal.

Beth was quiet now, and Louise hoped she was asleep. The girl needed the rest. Walking all night had blistered their feet and drained their strength.

They were headed west. At least Louise thought they were. She couldn't have said why, unless somewhere deep in her brain she was harboring the mad desire to catch up to Abner Clayborne and see that he paid for what he had done.

Someone laughed.

Louise's head jerked up, her eyes wide. She leaned forward and listened intently, trying to pick up the sound again. There was nothing, though. Had she only imagined it?

Dammit, no! She wasn't the type to imagine something like that. She was sure it had been real, a man's laugh, raucous and full of life. Carefully, she got to her feet.

There! It came again, floating to her ears on the hot air, followed this time by the sound of talking. More than one man, and they were coming closer.

The sun dazzled her eyes, and she lifted her hand to shade them. She turned her head toward the sound and squinted, barely making out movement. Three men on horses, she saw as her vision adjusted somewhat to the brightness. They were riding through the stubby little mesquite trees and leading strings of horses behind them.

Louise began to wave her arms in the air as she ran toward the men. Her throat was dry, and her first yell was little more than a croak. But then she regained her voice and called, "Help! Please, help!"

The three men reined in abruptly, shocked to see a

beautiful young woman running toward them in a gown that had once been expensive but was now tattered and dirty. The horses in the remuda they were leading began to shy nervously, and one of the men, a tall, thin cowboy wearing a pair of rimless spectacles, turned in his saddle and spoke soothingly to them. The animals quieted down.

Louise ran nearly all the way to the three cowboys before her legs failed her. Exhaustion had drained most of her strength, and when she felt herself falling there was nothing she could do to stop it. She went down on her knees, tearing her dress once again, and caught herself on her hands. Rocks bruised her palms, but she didn't feel them. She lifted her head, tears trying to run from her eyes, and regarded the young cowboys as if they were godlike beings.

The three men looked at the sobbing woman on her hands and knees and then glanced at each other, clearly at a loss what to do now.

The one slightly in the lead, a burly young man with a dark, closely trimmed beard, swung down out of the saddle and stepped forward, hesitating a bit as he held out a hand to Louise. "Let me help you up, ma'am," he said.

She took his hand and allowed him to haul her to her feet. She started to sag against him, and he caught her awkwardly before she could fall again. As he held her, he glanced over his shoulder and growled at his two companions still on horseback, "One of you get down and give a hand."

The third rider, a wiry individual with sandy hair and a quick, mocking grin, said dryly, "Looks to me like you're doin' mighty fine by yourself, Hemp."

"Dammit," the man called Hemp bit off, "you shut your trap and get down here, Lansford. You, too, Doc."

The other two cowboys dismounted and stepped up, whisking their hats off and nodding a greeting to Louise. The one called Doc said in a soft-spoken, intelligent voice, "We'd best get you into some shade, ma'am."

Louise turned slightly, grateful that Hemp was holding her up, and pointed back the way she had come. "My sister," she said in a little more than a gasp. "She's back there."

Hemp looked a command at Lansford, who said, "I'll go find her, boys." He leaped back into the saddle and spurred off.

Louise closed her eyes and leaned her head against Hemp's chest, making the cowboy look slightly uncomfortable and nervous. She wasn't aware of that and wouldn't have cared if she had been. One thought burned in her brain.

She was going to live.

Thirteen

*H*ank and Buffalo rode out of their camp the next morning before the sun was even touching the eastern horizon. The air was chilly, which helped Hank stay awake. His dream-haunted sleep hadn't been very restful.

Buffalo was singing as they rode out, and Hank didn't see how anybody could be so cheerful this early in the morning. The big man swayed in the saddle as the mule plodded along. Stink was riding in a burlap bag tied to the saddlehorn, his nose and tail protruding from holes cut in the bag. Evidently he was used to riding that way.

Buffalo had his pipe lit and was singing around the stem. He wore a black hat with a wide, floppy brim and had the Sharps tucked under his left arm. His voice rolled out over the plains as he sang. Hank didn't recognize any of the songs, and he supposed that they were the ones Buffalo had written. He remembered Buffalo promising—maybe threatening was a better word—to write one about him.

Buffalo came to the end of one tune and reached down to pet the possum through the sack. Stink twisted around, baring his teeth. "Want me to sing the one about you, eh? All right, ya smelly ol' varmint. Here goes.

> Oh, ride with me and I'll sing ya a song,
> A song of a stinkin' fool!
> It started late one rainy night
> Aboard this mighty ani-*mule!*
>
> He come a-waddlin' out of the storm,
> The night was black as ink!
> He was trailin' an awesome stench,
> And so I named him Stink,
> And so I named him Stink!
>
> Oh, possum is a filthy beast,
> As filthy as can be,
> The only beast I ever knew
> That stunk worse than me!
>
> We've been together since
>   that night,
> A-roamin' through the land,
> Just me and Stink and this ol' mule,
> A fierce and mighty band!
> A fierce and mighty band!"

The last words boomed out, Buffalo's voice seeming to expand until it stretched from horizon to horizon, filling the endless expanse of sky above. Clearly, this was one of his favorite songs.

Hank looked at him for a long moment, unsure of what to say. Buffalo kept glancing over at him, clearly waiting for some sort of response. Finally, Hank took a deep breath and said, "Don't reckon I've ever heard anything like that before."

"Course you ain't. It's a Buffalo Newcomb original. I'm workin' on one about you, boy. You just wait and see."

Waiting was all right with Hank.

Along about midmorning, they came to a small series of waterholes, grouped fairly close together. The vegetation was greener, more lush, around the springs. Buffalo reined in the mule.

"We'd best fill up our canteens," he said. "Out here, a man don't pass up the chance to take on water. Never know when the next hole might be dried up."

Hank got down from his horse and took the canteen that was looped around the saddlehorn over to the nearest waterhole. The water was muddy and murky, but in this part of the country a man couldn't afford to be too particular about things like that. As he knelt and began to fill the canteen, he said, "Have you been through here before?"

"Oh, hell, yes," Buffalo answered. "These are the Flat Rock Water Holes. Usually don't dry up until August or thereabouts. Filled my skins here many a time."

"Seems like you've been all over West Texas."

"Been roamin' around, man and boy, for nigh onto forty years, most of it west of the Brazos." Buffalo nodded sagely. "Been a few miles down the trail, all right, son."

Hank finished filling the canteen and thought how lucky he had been to run across Buffalo Newcomb. Of course, Buffalo was lucky he had come along, too, else those Apaches might have finished him off. Somehow, after getting to know the man, he doubted that.

Six Indians were no match for Buffalo Newcomb.

As they rode out, still headed west, there seemed to be no end to Buffalo's songs. After a while Hank got to where he could ignore them, just like he ignored the smell wafting from the big man. On the rare occasions when Buffalo fell silent, the quietness now disturbed Hank. He found himself asking questions to break up the monotony.

"I'm not sure why you're helping me," he said once.

"You could have gone on your way and left me back there."

Buffalo shook his head. "A man don't do things like that out here. You see an hombre in trouble, you just naturally try to help him out. 'Cause it might be your neck on the line someday, and he can help you then."

"Maybe so, but this morning you could have headed in any direction you wanted. I'm better now, able to take care of myself."

"Not so sure about that," Buffalo grunted. "But like I told you, boy, I'm just wanderin'. One direction's as good as another." Buffalo paused, then added cryptically, "Reckon there's one other reason, too."

"What?" Hank asked.

Buffalo didn't say anything for a long moment, and Hank began to wonder if he had pushed too far with his questioning. But then Buffalo said, "Had a family once. The boy would be your age now, the girl a little younger."

Hank frowned. "What happened to them?"

"I lost them," Buffalo said flatly.

"Oh. I'm sorry." Hank looked off at the horizon, wishing he had never started this conversation. It had to have brought back some painful memories for the big man.

"Hell, boy, stop your mopin'," Buffalo said sharply. "You don't understand. They ain't dead, I just don't recollect where I left 'em. Figure if I wander around long enough, maybe I'll run across 'em again." He shook his head. "It's a terrible thing to lose your family like that."

His voice was utterly sincere, and though Hank looked at him for a long time, he never could decide if Buffalo was lying about the whole thing.

Late that afternoon, Buffalo pointed a blunt finger at a smudge on the western horizon. "Dust," he said shortly.

"What does it mean?"

"Lots of horses movin' along, maybe a dozen or more. No way of knowin' who they belong to yet. Could be

Indians, could be white men. Hell, could even be a bunch of wild mustangs. But whatever it is, it's comin' this way.''

''Don't reckon it's anybody we want to meet,'' Hank said.

Buffalo squinted up at the sun. ''We won't meet up with 'em today. Ain't enough daylight left for that. Might be a good idea to sort of scout around tonight and find out just who they are. Don't like havin' a bunch of folks around without knowin' who they are.''

That made sense to Hank. If the dust was being kicked up by a band of Indians, that would be good to know. And if the group was made up of white men, they might be willing to share their fire and some coffee. He could even ask if they had met up with Abner Clayborne between here and El Paso.

He and Buffalo continued heading west, but they kept a close eye on the ever-growing dust cloud. By the time night had fallen, Buffalo estimated that only a mile or so separated them from the oncoming group.

Hank and Buffalo dismounted and waited until it was good and dark, then Buffalo said, ''You wait here with the animals. I'll go have me a look-see.'' His voice was pitched low, especially for him. Voices carried out here at night, so you had to be careful.

''I thought I'd go with you,'' Hank replied. He was holding the reins of their mounts and the packhorse.

''Somebody's got to watch them horses and my ol' mule. Any 'Paches come wanderin' along and find them animals with nobody around, and we'd be on foot 'fore you know it.''

What Buffalo was saying made sense, but that didn't mean Hank had to like it. Grudgingly he agreed to watch the horses.

''*Bueno*. I'll be back.''

Moving with more stealth and grace than Hank would have thought possible, Buffalo vanished into the shadowy brush.

Hank watched the spot where he had disappeared for several minutes. His eyes started to hurt, and he shifted his gaze to the winking eye of a campfire in the distance. It looked like a pretty good blaze, and by watching closely, he could see some figures moving around it. He felt a pang of regret somewhere deep inside, a sudden and fierce urge to return home, to be around people again.

Home wasn't the same now, though. Thomas was gone.

And Hank knew that he couldn't turn aside from this drive for revenge. Not yet.

Fingers dug hard into his shoulder, and a huge hand clamped itself over his mouth, stifling the cry that welled up in his throat.

"Take it easy, boy," Buffalo rasped. "It's just me. Was I a heathen you'd be dead right now. Best not to let your mind wander at night, or any other time, out here."

He took his hand away from Hank's mouth, leaving a bad taste behind. Hank spat, then said, "Did you see them?"

"Sure did. There's five people and a remuda of what looks like good saddle mounts." Buffalo paused, then said, "Two of 'em's women."

"Women?"

"Girls, more like. Purty li'l' things, one with yeller hair and one dark. The one with yeller hair don't look to be much older'n you. You know 'em?"

"What did the men look like?" he asked, his voice tight with anticipation.

"Just three young waddies," Buffalo said. "Don't reckon any of 'em are the men you're lookin' for. They don't look right, anyway."

Hank felt a keen surge of disappointment. However, just because the men weren't the ones he was looking for didn't mean that the girls weren't.

"I've got to get a look at them," he said.

"Figured you'd want to." Buffalo's teeth shone in the darkness as he grinned. "Come on. Might as well bring the horses. Them boys didn't look like anything we can't handle.''

They moved off into the night toward the campfire, leading the horses and Buffalo's mule.

Louise leaned against Hemp Morrison's saddle, a cup of coffee in her hand, and thought about how wonderful it was just to feel human again. Food and water and a little rest made all the difference in the world.

Beth was sitting on the other side of the fire, talking in low tones with Doc Williams. Earlier, he had put some salve on her back, and her strength seemed to be returning.

They had covered quite a bit of ground since the three cowboys had found them earlier in the day. Hemp was the nominal leader, and he pushed all of them, himself included, pretty hard. Louise's behind was sore tonight after riding bareback on one of the remuda much of the day. Beth had done the same. Both of them had worn blankets over their heads to block the sun. The cowboys had made several stops to let them rest and get out of the sun for a few minutes.

Hemp came around the fire and sat down cross-legged near her. He had a cup of coffee in his hand. He sighed, pushed his hat back, and sipped the hot, strong liquid.

"Where's your friend Mr. Lansford?" Louise asked. She didn't see him anywhere around the camp.

"Lop-Ear's around on the other side of the remuda, makin' sure they're all hobbled. We'll stand watches all night, but it don't hurt to make sure them brutes can't run off easy."

"Did he really bite someone's ear off?" she asked, recalling something one of them had said earlier.

Hemp grinned. "Damn right he did. Sunk his teeth in and ripped it right off. I was there."

"All of that over a dog?"

Hemp sipped his coffee again and then said, "He was always right fond of that dog. It was an ugly hound, but I reckon I miss it myself."

Louise made her tone sympathetic. "What happened to it?"

"Comanches," Hemp said shortly. "A raidin' party come through the Staked Plains. Got my ma and pa, Lansford's brother, Doc's aunt and uncle. That was all the family any of us had, so since we were on our own, we sort of drifted together and teamed up. Got a horse ranch we're tryin' to make something out of."

Louise smiled at him. "I hope you're very successful with it."

"We're workin' hard enough at it."

They were both quiet for a few moments, and Louise was aware that Hemp was casting glances at her out of the corner of his eye. She knew what he was thinking. She had seen that same look on the faces of more men than she cared to remember. He was shy, however; she could tell that as well. He probably wouldn't approach her tonight. Before they reached San Angelo, though . . .

Well, he seemed nice enough, even if he was a little grumpy sometimes. And he had helped save her life, and Beth's. She wouldn't mind.

She heard one of the horses in the remuda whinny, and suddenly there was an answer from the brush beyond the light from the fire. Hemp and Doc heard the same thing and reacted with a quickness that left Louise gasping.

Hemp dropped his coffee and rolled to the side, whipping out his holstered Colt in a blur of motion. Across the fire, Doc had pushed Beth down as he surged to his feet, and there was also a gun in his hand. Both men looked around, ready to meet any threat that might come.

"Just stand easy, boys," a booming voice said. "They's a Sharps and a Henry pointin' right at you, and we don't want to go blowin' holes in nobody."

Hemp and Doc didn't lower their guns. "Step out where we can see you," Hemp called.

"And do it quick," a new voice put in from the brush off to one side. Lansford had noticed that something was wrong, too.

"We don't want any gunplay," the booming voice replied. "Go easy on them triggers, boys. We're comin' out."

Two figures stepped from the shadows into the circle of light. Both of them held rifles and were ready to use them. The one in the lead was a massive, bearded man in a battered black hat and a blanket poncho. The big Sharps almost looked small in his hands. He was followed by a tall, broad-shouldered young man with blond hair and an honest, open face. He didn't look too threatening until you saw the way he held the Henry.

Beth was half lying on the ground where Doc Williams had shoved her so that she would be out of the line of fire. She looked up at the strangers, and her eyes locked on the face of the young man.

She screamed.

She scuttled backward, using her hands and feet to propel her, losing her balance and falling. Her hands came up to her face to cover her eyes as she continued to scream, piercing shrieks that hurt the ears. Louise ran to her side, careful not to get in front of Hemp and Doc in case shooting started.

Louise fell to her knees beside Beth and tried to gather the younger girl into her arms. Beth struck out blindly at her. "Nooo! Get away!" Beth cried. "He's not going to take me, I won't let him take me!"

Louise caught Beth's wrists and forced her arms down.

Beth ripped one hand free of Louise's grasp and pointed, wide-eyed, at the blond young man. "He's come back for me," she wavered. "He's a ghost! Nooo!"

Louise glanced at the man and felt her own heart start to pound. She recognized him now, all right. The old man's grandson, the one who had helped with the coffin. . . .

The last time she had seen him, Reuben Reed and Ignacio Jiménez had been carrying his body away.

Maybe Beth was right, Louise thought wildly. Maybe he was a ghost.

"All right, you two, what the hell's this all about?" Hemp Morrison demanded in a harsh voice. The potential for sudden violence still hung heavily in the air.

"Name's Buffalo Newcomb," the big man said. "This here's Hank Littleton—"

Beth let out another muffled shriek, and Louise remembered that was indeed the name of the sheriff's grandson.

Buffalo went on, "We been lookin' for these two ladies." He hadn't been too sure that busting into the camp was a good idea, but once Hank had seen who the two young women were, there wasn't any holding him back.

"They're under our protection," Doc said quietly.

"We don't want to hurt them," Hank said suddenly, speaking up for the first time. "We just want to talk."

Louise studied Hank's grim face, and a flash of intuition suddenly burst on her. "You're after Abner, aren't you?" she asked, unable to hold the question in.

Hank nodded. "Yes, ma'am, we are. Don't reckon it'd do any good to lie to you."

Hemp glanced over at Louise. "You know these two varmints?" he asked.

"I know the younger one," Louise replied. Beth had settled down somewhat, but she was still breathing raggedly and watching Hank like he was some sort of demon about to attack her and possess her soul. Louise went on, "I don't think we have anything to fear from them."

"I just want Clayborne," Hank said simply. He let the muzzle of the Henry dip toward the ground. Buffalo glanced at him, grimaced slightly, and did the same with the Sharps.

Hemp and Doc eased a bit, though they kept their guns up, and Lansford stepped out of the brush on the other side of the camp. He had his Colt out as well.

Hemp said thoughtfully, "Sounds to me like you're lookin' for the same man who left these ladies out here to die. So maybe we're on the same side of the fence after all. Just don't go gettin' any ideas about makin' a play.''

Hank shook his head. He had moved up a step in front of Buffalo now. "I just want to talk to them.''

When he came still closer, Beth clutched at Louise and whimpered. Louise looked at Doc and said, "Mr. Williams, would you mind seeing to my sister? And don't you come any closer, mister. Can't you see you're scaring her?''

Hank stopped and mumbled an apology. He was holding the rifle loosely at his side now, and the crisis seemed to have passed for the moment.

Doc holstered his gun and came around the fire to Beth's side. He knelt and took her arm, helped her to her feet. She sagged against him, but he held her up effortlessly and assisted her away from the others.

Hemp stepped up to Buffalo and eyed the big man with the scarred face. He still had his Colt in his hand, but it was at his side now. "Mind tellin' me what's goin' on here?'' he asked.

"That's up to the boy,'' Buffalo grunted.

Hank glanced over at Doc and Beth and then pitched his voice low enough that they couldn't hear him. He didn't want to upset Beth anymore than he already had.

"How much have you told them?'' he asked Louise.

"Just that Abner abandoned us out here. The others went along with him, of course. You know why.'' She obviously didn't want to mention the gold.

"Why did he do that?''

"He's insane,'' Louise said coldly. "Beth was upset ever since we . . . ever since we left San Saba.''

The muscles in Hank's jaw tightened, but he kept the emotions he was feeling under control.

"She pulled a gun on Abner,'' Louise went on. "He went berserk, whipped her. Then he said he was leaving us. I didn't believe he really would, but as you can see, he did.''

"You knew what he was going to do to my grand-father," Hank accused.

"Let's say I suspected. Abner has always done just what he wanted. There's no stopping him."

Hank lifted the rifle. "I'm going to stop him."

"Only if you find him first. You knew they were going to El Paso?"

Hank nodded. "I was hoping to find the whole bunch of you there."

"I'm going with you." It was a simple declaration, and Louise's tone said that she would tolerate no argument. "I can help you find him."

"Wait just a goldurn minute," Buffalo put in. "I didn't reckon on totin' no female along with us, Hank."

"You think I'd trust you?" Hank asked her. "After the things you've done? I might wake up some morning with a knife in my back."

Louise shook her head. "I don't have anything against you. It was all Abner's doing, I tell you. All I want is to see him get what's coming to him."

Lansford spoke up. "We can't take you to El Paso, ma'am. You know we got to get them horses to San Angelo."

"Our ranch is ridin' on sellin' those critters," Hemp agreed. "We can't turn around now."

"I'm not asking you to," Louise told the two cowboys. "I know you have to sell the horses. In fact, I want to buy a couple of them from you."

"No." Hank shook his head vehemently, before Hemp could reply. "You're not going with us."

"I don't think you can trust 'em, ma'am," Lansford commented to Louise. "They look like mean 'uns."

"You're a fine one to talk about that, Lop-Ear." Hemp got the dig in out of habit. He turned back to Louise. "Anyway, ma'am, how would you pay for the horses?"

Unashamed, Louise lifted the hem of her dress and reached underneath it. Hank turned his head away, embarrassed, as did Hemp and Lansford. Buffalo looked appreciatively at her calves and knees.

She thrust the wad of currency toward Hemp as she let her dress drop back into place. No one, not even Abner, had known that she had it.

"There's more there than what you'll get in San Angelo for the whole herd," she said. "All I want for it is two good horses."

To her surprise, Hemp peeled off a couple of the bills and then offered the rest back to her. "This's a fair price," he said gruffly. "That's all we want."

"You're sure?"

Hemp nodded, pressing the money back into her hands. "You can't start out tonight, though," he said. "Come mornin', we'll cut you out a couple of good saddle broncs. In the meantime, you gents had supper?"

Hank and Buffalo admitted that they hadn't, and Hemp offered them the hospitality of the camp. "Thankee," Buffalo said with a nod.

He went to get their animals, which they had left tied up just outside the camp. When he returned, the others saw the possum trailing along behind him. Lansford reached for his pistol, saying, "Look at that! Possum stew, boys!"

Before his fingers could touch the butt of his Colt, he found himself staring down the barrel of the Sharps. It looked as big and dark as a cave.

"Never did care for possum stew myself," Buffalo rasped.

Lansford slowly shook his head. "Reckon I don't either."

Beth and Doc were still staying well away from the others. Her crying was under control now, but Beth was still staring with big eyes at Hank. As he hunkered by the fire, drinking coffee and enjoying the bread and salt pork, he said to Louise, "I didn't mean to scare your sister."

"I know you didn't. She's just had a rough time of it

this year. Our parents died, and then she had the journey from Georgia with the rest of us. . . ."

"Sorry about your folks," Hank grunted.

"I . . . hadn't seen them in years. Anyway, she's just had too many shocks." She smiled tiredly. "By the way, I'm Louise Shelby. Her name is Beth."

"Hank Littleton." His mouth twisted. "But you know that."

"Yes."

Buffalo was tearing into the food with even more enthusiasm than Hank, pausing occasionally to flip a piece to Stink. Usually the food would bounce off the animal's nose, and then he would have to find it again with his sense of smell before he could devour it almost whole. "Told you the critter couldn't hardly see," Buffalo chuckled.

Hank finished his meal and picked up his coffee, carrying it around the fire to where Beth and Doc were sitting. Beth watched him closely, but she didn't cry out.

"Howdy, Miss Shelby," Hank said. He was well aware that the others were watching him, especially Louise. "I'm sorry I scared you earlier, and I just wanted to tell you that."

"You . . . you're not a ghost," Beth whispered.

"No, ma'am, I'm surely not."

"I saw them shoot you."

"That's a fact, ma'am. I reckon I was lucky."

Beth swallowed. "They shot Ignacio. We covered his body with rocks."

Hank glanced over at Louise. She hadn't told him about that. "I'm sorry to hear that. Was he your friend?"

"Oh, yes," Beth nodded. "He was a good man, I think. He just didn't know what to do. He tried to help me, and Mr. Clayborne shot him."

In a quiet voice, Doc said, "I don't know if she should be talking about this, son—"

"No, it's all right," Beth said suddenly. She blinked and shook her head. When she looked up at Hank, her eyes were clearer, her expression more alert. "I need to."

Hank knelt so that their eyes would be on the same level. "Did you see what they did with my grandfather's body?"

Beth nodded slowly. "They dressed him in a uniform, a Confederate uniform, and then they put him in the coffin. Abner was going to tell people that he was his uncle."

It was starting to make some sense to Hank now.

"They . . . they threw him in a gully." Beth closed her eyes. "It was awful. I couldn't let Louise stay with those terrible men anymore."

Hank looked at Louise, saw the expression on her face, and knew that Beth was telling the truth. Louise said, "I couldn't find the place again. I'm sorry."

"I could find it," Beth declared.

"You couldn't," Louise insisted. "You were out of your head with the pain when we were walking. . . ."

"I could find it."

"Maybe when this is over," Hank said. "Maybe we'll look for the place then."

Buffalo and the three cowboys had listened intently to the conversation, knowing that there was a great deal of drama behind it without knowing the details. Buffalo drew a flask out from under his poncho, poured a healthy dollop of whiskey into his coffee and passed the liquor on to Hemp, who sent it around the circle. Buffalo downed the spiked coffee, then looked from face to face. He shook his head.

"Damned if this ain't the gloomiest bunch I ever did see," he boomed. "What you folks need is a song!"

Hank closed his eyes and started to laugh. . . .

"Y'all ever heard 'The Ballad of Buffalo Newcomb'? I didn't think so!"

Fourteen

Enos Littleton was damned tired. He had ridden nearly all the way across West Texas, and so far hadn't even found the ghost of a trail.

Now, as he reined in on top of a small rise, he could look to the southwest and see the winding ribbon of the Rio Grande. On the other side of the river rose the mountains of Mexico, and below, nestled on both banks of the river, was a small town. Enos wasn't sure what it was called, but knew it wasn't El Paso. El Paso del Norte was still a good two days' ride upriver.

He put the horse down the slope, anxious to be around people again. And maybe someone here had spotted the men he was seeking.

As the sun dipped below the crest of the mountains on the other side of the border, Enos heard music coming from the town. Chords from a softly strummed guitar and words sung caressingly, liquidly, in Spanish drifted to his ears on the early evening air. He followed the sounds to a cantina, figuring that pretty music like that might have drawn a crowd.

He had figured correctly, he saw as he swung down

and hitched the horse at a rail outside the squat adobe building. There were quite a few horses tied there, and several men lounged in the open doorway. Some were Mexican and some were white, but they all had the same lean stamp.

Border wolves. Smugglers. *Bandidos*.

He was almost glad he had lost his Ranger badge back in Eagle Cove. That silver star on a silver circle was instantly recognizable, and if he had accidently dropped it in a place like this, it would get him shot in a hurry.

The men in the doorway were passing a bottle back and forth, laughing and joking. They didn't seem to be paying any attention to Enos as he walked closer, but he knew their eyes were actually sweeping over him and trying to decide what he was made of.

The inside of the cantina was crowded too. The rough tables scattered around on the packed earth floor were mostly full. Every table had at least one bottle of tequila or mescal on it. The bar to one side was thronged with men. Through the crowd moved serving girls in long skirts and low-cut white blouses that left shoulders and a great deal of their breasts bare.

In the corner opposite the bar, a *vaquero* in gaudy clothes played the guitar while a lovely young girl with long raven hair sang. It was she whom Enos had heard, and her songs were even more enchanting now that he could hear them clearly. He had enough Spanish to follow the lyrics and knew that, as usual, they were filled with passion and heartbreak. The gown the girl wore was silk, a bright red decorated with intricate beadwork, and a tall red comb was in her midnight hair. Altogether, she belonged someplace other than a squalid little cantina.

He found a place at the crowded bar and called over the hubbub of noise, "Beer, *por favor!*"

One of the sweating bartenders filled a mug and slid it over in front of him. Enos flipped the man a coin, then sampled the beer. It was warm, but at least it cut the trail dust in his mouth.

The man next to him, a big Mexican, jostled his arm and made Enos slosh some of the beer out onto his hand. Enos glanced at the man, anger rising in him. He caught himself as he realized that the man hadn't even noticed the incident. Forcing the anger back down, he resumed sipping the beer.

He didn't want to call attention to himself. That wouldn't help his mission at all.

Instinct told him he was being watched. He glanced over his shoulder and saw three *vaqueros* sitting at a nearby table. All of them were grinning, and he supposed that they had observed the way he had let the bumping incident slide. As they spoke among themselves in low voices and began to laugh, he wondered if he had made a mistake.

In a place like this, being a peaceable man could draw just as much attention as making trouble.

Enos looked back at the bar and wished there was a mirror behind it so he could keep track of what was going on. He heard chairs being pushed back behind him, and he had a feeling that the three *vaqueros* were getting to their feet. Resisting the temptation to look over his shoulder again, he lifted the mug of beer to his lips.

A hand smacked into his back, jarring him forward. The beer splashed up into his face. "Amigo!" boomed the man.

Enos lifted his left hand and wiped the dripping beer from his face. He put the mug down on the bar and turned half around, all too aware that he was leaving his back exposed to some of the other men at the bar.

Just as he had thought, the three men who had been watching him had moved up to the bar, closing him in against it. They had seen him ignore the earlier affront, and now they were going to have some fun with him.

Enos just wished they would go away. He wasn't in any mood for it.

"Did you spill your drink, amigo?" the biggest of the trio asked. His clothes were worn and patched, and his boots and sombrero had seen better days, but the gun belt around his waist was fine leather, obviously made by a master craftsman. The other two looked much the same. All three men were lean, dark-featured, mustachioed.

Enos tried to smile and was only partially successful. "Reckon I'm clumsy," he replied. "No harm done, though."

"This is good," the man nodded sagely. "You could have spilled the whole thing."

His hand flicked out and hit the mug, knocking it over and spilling the rest of the beer on the bar. It puddled and then ran, dripping off the hardwood onto Enos's boots.

Slowly, Enos moved his feet so that the trickle of beer would miss them, then he reached over with his left hand and grasped the overturned mug. He shot a glance back at the Mexican behind him, then let his eyes move to the one on his right. The leader, the one who seemed the most intent on tormenting him, was right in front of him.

The man shook his head. "Such a shame," he said sadly. The other two were grinning wickedly and trying to suppress outright laughter at this gringo they were cowing so easily.

"Damned shame, all right," Enos agreed.

The guitar player reached the end of the tune and finished with a crescendo of notes, accompanied by the singer's soulful tones.

Without looking, Enos slammed the beer mug in his left hand into the face of the man behind him. His right hand blurred as his Colt came out. The Mexican he had hit screamed as he staggered backward, his hands over his bloody, ruined face. The other two grabbed for their guns.

Twin blasts cut across the screaming as the other patrons of the bar scrambled for safety. The two *vaqueros* jerked back as Enos's bullets took them. The leader got his pistol out of its holster before it slipped from nerveless fingers. The other man didn't even come that close. Both of them folded up onto the earthen floor and lay still, their blood draining out into the dust.

Silence dropped over the cantina as the shots exploded, and in the quiet as the echoes died away, Enos heard a sound behind him. He whirled and saw that the other man had gotten his gun out. His face was awash with blood where the mug had shattered and he couldn't see clearly. His first shot went wild, thumping into the thick adobe wall.

Enos triggered his Colt.

The man dropped, still holding his free hand over his face. His feet jerked spasmodically for a second, then he was still.

Enos turned around, putting his back to the bar, and surveyed the room, his gun still up and ready. Everyone in the place was staring at him, but no one moved.

"Señor," the bartender croaked, "do you know who it is you have killed?"

"Nope," Enos answered without turning around.

"The big one there, he is Pablo Garzón. And you have killed him." The man sounded awestruck.

"He called the tune," Enos said flatly. "Who is he, some local badman?" The name was vaguely familiar to Enos, but he couldn't place it.

"He is—was—a bandit, *sí*. Also the brother of the *jefe* of Ciudad Juárez."

Enos frowned. Brother of the mayor of Juárez, eh? The facts came back to him now. Pablo Garzón was indeed the local badman. In fact, he controlled just about everything that was lawless in this end of the state. Smuggling, murder, stage holdups, what have you . . . Pablo Garzón had a finger in it.

And that was who Enos had picked to shoot.

A slight smile pulled at the corner of his mouth.

He had been proddy from being on the trail so long. Now all he could do was hope that he hadn't thrown too big an obstacle in his own path.

"Anybody goin' to object if I walk out of here?" he asked the room in general.

The barman answered, "Please, señor, I wish you would. Dead bodies, they are bad for business."

The grim smile still on his face, Enos made his way toward the door. He was afraid there would be trouble, since he couldn't look in all directions at once, but no one made a move to stop him. As he reached the doorway, he took a look back at the crowded room and felt one pair of eyes watching him with a special intensity.

The raven-haired singer in the corner. She was the one whose gaze was boring in on him. His eyes met hers for a second, but he couldn't read those fathomless dark eyes. He couldn't tell if she was happy or sad that Pablo Garzón was dead. Maybe she felt nothing at all about it.

Enos ducked through the door, hurried to his horse, mounted up, and rode quickly away from there. He didn't holster his gun until the lights of the settlement were far behind him.

Fifteen

Abner Clayborne hauled back on the lines and brought the Conestoga's team to a halt. His back and shoulders ached with weariness from driving all day. He had wanted to reach El Paso today. Even though the little group was still several miles out of town as darkness fell, Clayborne had insisted that they push on.

Now, as the two wagons came to a halt in front of the Hotel Camino, Clayborne felt a great sense of relief. The longest leg of his journey was over. Soon he would meet the man called Espinoza, and they could plan the final stretch of the trip.

Reuben Reed was tired, too, and he was looking forward to the opportunity to sleep in a bed again. The Hotel Camino might not be the most luxurious accommodations in the world, but it looked damn good to him at the moment. He jumped heavily from the box of the second wagon and walked up next to the Conestoga.

"Now what, Abner?" he asked Clayborne.

"Go inside and let them know that we've arrived."

Ordway and Smith had ridden up next to the Conestoga on the other side. They were used to spending a lot of time in the saddle, but even they were showing signs of the strain generated by this trip. They waited while Reed went into the hotel, then Clayborne turned to them.

"One of you is to have that coffin in your sight at all times," he said. "I don't intend to let it out of my sight, either, but there may be times when I have to. You know to kill anyone who tries to tamper with it."

"We know," Ordway said flatly.

Clayborne's grim expression eased somewhat. "You men have done a good job," he said.

"We're being paid well," Ordway replied.

"I haven't forgotten that."

Inside the hotel, Reed went up to the desk in the lobby and said to the clerk, "Mr. Clayborne's party has arrived. I believe we have reservations."

The clerk was a tall young man in a sober black suit. He looked more like a church deacon than a hotel clerk. He smiled noncommittally and said, "Clayborne? I'll look it up." The clerk found the notation in his records, and his smile became considerably more genuine. "Yes, indeed. We're holding three rooms for you, Mr. Clayborne."

"I'm not Clayborne, and we'll only need two rooms," Reed said. "Some of our group didn't come after all."

Thoughts of Louise and Beth alone out on the plains intruded into Reed's head. He usually tried not to think about the girls. Surely they were dead by now. It had been almost a week since they had been abandoned. Either the heat, or thirst, or wild animals would have killed them.

It didn't do any good to feel guilty about them, Reed told himself. If he had tried to interfere, Clayborne might well have killed him, too, just like he had coldly shot the Mexican. Abner Clayborne was one man who did what he wanted, regardless of who got hurt or whether or not it made sense. Like that coffin business. Reed liked the idea of the gold being hidden, but why in a coffin? He had a feeling that the gold bars would always carry the stench of death on them.

The clerk turned the register around and pushed it across the desk to Reed. He held out a quill pen. "Would you care to sign for Mr. Clayborne?"

Reed took the pen and scratched *Abner Clayborne and party*. "I assume our rooms are ready now," he said.

"Yes, indeed, sir. I'll have a boy help you."

Reed shook his head. "That's all right. We'll handle our bags." Clayborne had given orders that no one was to get near the coffin or anything else in the wagons.

"Well . . . all right," the clerk agreed, somewhat surprised. He took two keys from the rack behind him and extended them to Reed. He went on apologetically, "You understand, of course, that we'll have to charge you for the third room, but only for the days that we actually held it."

"Fine, fine," Reed said. He took the keys and turned back to the door, anxious to find out how Clayborne wanted to proceed from here.

"All taken care of?" Clayborne asked when Reed came back out onto the porch.

"Here are the keys." Reed handed them over and then asked, "What were you planning on doing with the coffin?"

"There's a stable down the street. We'll leave the wagons there. They shouldn't be there any longer than tonight, and we can guard them for that long."

Reed suppressed a groan. "You mean we're not going to stay here in the hotel?"

"We'll take turns, Reuben. Don't worry, you'll get some rest." Clayborne's tone was mildly contemptuous.

El Paso *was* jumping. Several of the stores were still open for business, even at this late hour, and there were wagons and buckboards tied up in front of them. Customers went back and forth on the sidewalks, loading their supplies.

The saloons were even busier. The noise from several

different establishments came through the batwinged entrances and blended into one chaotic sound in the street, punctuated occasionally by the blast of a gunshot.

"We'll take the wagons down to the stable now," Clayborne said. "Then you and Bob can come back and get some sleep. Gus and I will watch over our cargo."

Reed nodded and climbed onto the box of the second wagon. He and Clayborne got the teams moving, driving carefully down the street to the stable.

A middle-aged Mexican and two young men who looked like his sons met them at the big doors. The older man swept off his sombrero and grinned up at Clayborne. "Hello, señor," he said. "You wish a place to keep your wagons and animals?"

"That is exactly what I wish," Clayborne replied.

"I am Benito Jiménez, the owner of this humble building, and I and my sons will do our best to serve you."

Reed jerked involuntarily when he heard the name. He had heard Ignacio Jiménez speak of having relatives in El Paso. It was possible that this stableman was one of them. On the other hand, Jiménez was a common enough name.

The young men unhitched the teams and put them in stalls, then came over to the wagons and stopped to stare at the coffin. One of them wrinkled his nose and said something in rapid-fire Spanish to his father.

Jiménez shot a reply back, then turned to Clayborne and said, "My sons, they worry about the, ah, the coffin. I think they fear the spirit of the departed."

"No need for that," Clayborne said heartily. "I can promise you, there's nothing in that coffin that can harm anyone."

"*Sí,* I understand, señor. But my sons are young. They hear the stories of the old women about ghosts, and sometimes they believe, though they would never admit it."

"Tell them not to worry. One of my men and I will be

here all night." Clayborne smiled. "Nothing will get out of that coffin. Nothing."

Clayborne handed over part of the payment, then said, "There is one thing you can do for us, Señor Jiménez. Do you know a man named Espinoza?"

"The *embalsamador? Sí,* everyone in El Paso knows him." Jiménez nodded in understanding. "You wish to speak with him, I am sure."

"Yes, I do. Could you send for him and have him meet me here?"

Jiménez shrugged. "Espinoza is a busy man, as you can well imagine. But I will send one of my sons to his place of business. If he is there, I am sure he will come."

"Thank you." Clayborne took an extra coin from his pocket and gave it to Jiménez. "For your son."

"*Sí, gracias.* Paco!" Jiménez gave his son a few words of instruction, and the young man nodded and hurried out of the stable.

Clayborne turned to Reed and said, "I believe everything is under control here, Reuben. Why don't you and Bob go get some sleep?"

"All right," Reed agreed. "I can use it." He frowned and went on, "There's just one thing I'm wondering about, Abner. This fellow Espinoza . . . I don't think I've heard you mention him before. What does he have to do with us?"

Clayborne smiled thinly. "I didn't deem it necessary to tell you *every* detail of my plan, Reuben. Señor Espinoza is a vital person to know in our situation."

Reed glanced at Jiménez, who had gone into the stable's tack room with his other son. "What was that the Mexican said about him? What's an *embalsamador?*"

"Just what we need, Reuben." Clayborne's smile became more smug. "An undertaker, my good man, an undertaker."

*   *   *

Clayborne stood beside the wagon containing the coffin. The lingering smell didn't bother him, because he knew what was underneath the false bottom. He rested a hand on the side of the wagon. Soon they would be in Mexico. Soon the gold would go to work building him a new empire.

Gus Ordway stood nearby, rolling a cigarette. "You trust that Mexican?" he said, inclining his head toward the tack room.

"He won't cause us any trouble," Clayborne said with confidence. "He's like all the other people on this side of the river. He knows how much power Espinoza has. No, Señor Jiménez won't do anything to get on Espinoza's bad side."

"Seems like I've heard of this Espinoza hombre. You told Reed he was an undertaker. I seem to remember him as a smuggler."

Clayborne smiled. "Señor Espinoza does a lucrative business burying people on both sides of the border. Many times, in fact, he has to transport a coffin from one side of the river to the other. And who would think to look inside a coffin for contraband?"

Ordway's eyes narrowed as he lit his quirly. He had started to think Clayborne was a little crazy, too, what with all this coffin business. Now, he saw that everything Clayborne had done had been for a purpose.

Maybe that was why Abner Clayborne was such a dangerous man.

A few minutes later, Paco Jiménez came back into the stable, slightly winded. He glanced at Clayborne and Ordway, then went to the tack room and spoke to his father in a low voice. Jiménez nodded as he came out of the room and went over to the wagons.

"Paco has spoken to Señor Espinoza, who has said that he will be here shortly. If it is all right with you, señor, my sons and I will go to our house now. I do not think my stable will have any other customers tonight. Our house, it is out back, close but not within earshot, so I would appreciate it if you would summon me should someone else require my services.''

"Of course, sir. I will be glad to." Clayborne knew quite well what Jiménez was actually saying. The stableman was going on record as being completely uninterested in whatever business Clayborne was going to discuss with Espinoza. That was the way both of them wanted it.

Five minutes after Jiménez and his sons had left the stable, someone tapped at the big main doors. Clayborne slipped his little pistol out of its holster and motioned for Ordway to answer the knock. Ordway drew his own gun as he went to the door. He worked the latch and swung one side open.

Outside was a carriage drawn by two horses. One man sat in the carriage, and as the entrance widened, he flicked the lines against his team and drove into the stable. He wore a dark suit and a white shirt, and a tall black hat was on his head. His face was lean to the point of gauntness, and his mouth was just a thin slash across the bottom part of his face. When he brought the carriage to a stop and climbed down from the seat, his great height was revealed. He swept the hat off his head, exposing a gleaming bald skull.

"Mr. Clayborne?" he asked in an accentless voice.

"I'm Abner Clayborne. You're Señor Espinoza?"

"Hernando Espinoza, sir, at your service. It is good to finally meet you face to face."

"And you, sir," Clayborne returned. He motioned to Ordway, who shut the door again. Clayborne went on, "I've heard a great deal about you, señor. They say that you know everyone in El Paso and Juárez who is worth knowing."

Espinoza smiled and spread his hands. "Everyone comes to me sooner or later. This is true."

"They also say that you can get anyone or anything across the border, either way. Is that true?"

"It is."

"In my letter, I asked you for an introduction to a man on the other side of the border who could provide what I need," Clayborne said. "Have you located such a man?"

Espinoza turned his hat over in his hands and suddenly looked nervous. "Knowing the identity of such a man is not difficult. Knowing where to find him sometimes can be. I understand that you need protection and men to ride with you as guides, that you wish to purchase a large hacienda. There is a man who could attend to these things for you. Unfortunately . . ."

Clayborne felt his heart begin to pound harder. "Is there some trouble?" he asked tightly. It would be just like a robber like Espinoza to demand that his cut be raised.

"I was supposed to meet this man today," Espinoza said. "He was to come to my office in Mexico. I have offices on both sides of the river," he added proudly.

"What happened?" Clayborne asked, impatient with the man's self-congratulations.

Espinoza shook his head. "He did not show up. I have had men out all afternoon and evening since then, trying to find out where he is or what has delayed him. But so far, I have heard nothing."

"Then there must be someone else who can do the same things," Clayborne suggested.

Once again, Espinoza slowly, ponderously shook his head. "I am sorry, señor. There is no one else who would dare take on such authority for themselves. I am afraid that on the other side of the border, the word of Pablo Garzón is law, and no one will proceed without it."

Obviously, Espinoza meant what he said. Clayborne took a deep breath and didn't say anything for a long moment. He spent the time mentally cursing this Pablo Garzón.

"What do I do, then?" he finally asked. "I've got to get these wagons and this coffin across the river and on into Mexico. Are you sure there's no one else?"

Espinoza shrugged. "Perhaps there will be. A man like

Garzón always has enemies. To be perfectly honest about it, someone may have killed him. If that is the case, a man will step forward eventually to take his place, but who knows how long that may take?''

Clayborne clenched his fist and drove it into the palm of his other hand. Anger and impatience gnawed at his belly. "Can you find whoever will take his place?''

"Sí," Espinoza said solemnly. "It will take a little time, though. I will hurry things as much as I can.''

"Do the best you can," Clayborne said, trying to keep the dissatisfaction out of his voice. It wouldn't be a good idea to be too rude to Espinoza; the man had a lot of power and influence here in El Paso.

"Of course," Espinoza nodded. "I am truly sorry, señor. This thing is not my fault, though.''

"I know it's not." Clayborne held out his hand and was glad when Espinoza took it for a moment. "I'll be either here or at the Hotel Camino.''

"I will be in touch," Espinoza said. He got into the carriage again, and as Ordway opened the doors, he backed the team out, turning the vehicle around and vanishing into the night.

"That plays hob with our plans," Ordway said as he shut the doors.

"We'll just have to change our plans," Clayborne snapped. For one thing, he thought, he couldn't stay with the coffin twenty-four hours a day. He had to sleep sometime. He had been prepared to stay with it all night tonight, but if that stretched out over several days, as Espinoza indicated, he couldn't hold up that long.

He would just have to trust the other three, Clayborne decided. He had no choice. Besides, they knew him well enough by now to know that if anyone double-crossed him, he would hunt that person down and kill him.

Slowly and painfully.

Sixteen

Traveling with Buffalo Newcomb was an experience, Hank thought. In addition to the endless stream of bawdy songs and jokes, Buffalo seemed to know everything there was to know about life on the frontier. He had been all over this territory and knew every landmark and the story behind its name. As they rode he would point out the plants that were edible and the ones that weren't. Hank learned how to get water from a barrel cactus and how to figure out where they were from the position of the stars at night.

And though Buffalo was no shootist, he watched Hank practicing with the Remington and gave him several valuable tips that speeded up his draw. At Buffalo's suggestion, Hank raised his holster slightly and filed off the weapon's front sight so that there was no chance of it hanging up.

When it came to rifles, there wasn't much the big man could teach him, though. There was no doubt that Buffalo's Sharps had more power than the Henry, but for sheer accuracy, the two of them were equally matched.

As long as the range wasn't too great, Hank could duplicate any shot that Buffalo made.

If not for the fact that they were on a mission of revenge, Hank thought more than once, he would almost be enjoying this journey.

Louise and Beth Shelby were constant reminders of why they were all here, though. Abner Clayborne was never far from Hank's mind.

Often as they rode along, Hank found himself stealing glances at Louise. Even with her dress dusty and torn and her hair tangled, he thought she was still the prettiest woman he had ever seen. But he had to admit that Beth was attractive, too. She would never have the glamour that Louise could achieve under better circumstances, but there was an innocent beauty about her that Louise could never regain.

Hank didn't know why he was thinking such damned foolish thoughts about either one of them. Louise didn't even know he was alive most of the time, and anyway she was too old for him. And Beth was still scared of him and looked at him like he was a ghost.

They made camp at a place Buffalo called Ellis Waterhole, which was in a rock-strewn bowl a little lower than the surrounding prairie. The trees that grew around it were a bit larger than the stunted mesquite, and they provided a welcome spot of shade. The grass around the spring was thicker and more green. It looked mighty cool and restful compared to the sparse, brown growth out on the plains. Much of the terrain now was just dirt, rock, and scrub brush.

Hank and Buffalo unsaddled the horses and the mule while the two women drank at the spring and topped off the canteens. None of them were very hungry, so they made a cold supper of jerky and cornbread left over from that morning. Buffalo built a small fire for coffee, then put it out so that the pot could stay warm all night in the ashes.

As Hank sat cross-legged on the ground, he sipped

from a tin cup of coffee and looked across the embers at Beth Shelby. She was gnawing determinedly on a piece of jerky.

"Reckon that's a mite tough," Hank said to her.

Beth paused long enough to say, "It's fine."

"Of course, jerky's supposed to be tough." As soon as he said it, Hank thought how stupid it sounded. He didn't have a lot of experience talking to females, though, and something about it sort of made him nervous and uncertain what to say. When you came right down to it, he hadn't ever had much to do with girls except for Rose Ellen Hobbs, and he had avoided her most of the time.

On the other side of the little camp, Buffalo watched and listened to the two young people and chuckled. Louise watched, too. She knew full well what was going on. She had seen the way Hank looked at Beth, and she had seen the glances he gave *her*.

She could wrap Hank Littleton around her little finger. Beth could have, too, if only she had known what to do.

Beth didn't know, though, so whatever would have to be done, Louise would have to do it.

Hank was trying unsuccessfully to think of something else to say, but when he couldn't come up with anything, he stared down into his coffee cup and felt foolish.

Buffalo finished his coffee and stood up, stretching. "Reckon I'll go scout around some."

"I'll go with you," Hank said eagerly as he got to his feet.

"No, you won't, boy. Somebody needs to stay here in camp with the womenfolk, and I reckon you're elected. 'Sides, you ain't got the knack o' walkin' quiet yet."

Hank flushed in anger and embarrassment. Buffalo had no call to talk to him that way. Also, calling him boy was starting to annoy him. There was no use arguing with him, though. Once Buffalo made up his mind about something, there was no changing it.

"All right," Hank said grudgingly. "I'll be here."

Buffalo nodded and faded away into the shadows.

Hank was still surprised every time he saw how quietly the big man could move.

Well, he couldn't just sit there like a lump of dirt. "Would you like some more coffee, Miss Beth?" he asked.

Beth shook her head. She swallowed the last of the jerky and took a drink from one of the canteens, then said, "I'm tired. I'm going to go to sleep." She took one of the blankets that Buffalo and Hank had given them and drew back under one of the trees. She spread the blanket there and lay down on it, turning her back to Hank and Louise. In a few minutes, the sound of her deep, regular breathing came to them.

Louise stood up and walked over to where Hank was sitting. She sank down on the ground there, gracefully tucking her legs underneath her. Hank watched her, and in the moonlight, she could see that his eyes were wide with surprise.

"I've been wanting to speak privately with you, Hank," Louise said softly.

"With me, Miss Louise?"

"Yes. And call me Louise, if you will. I'm not *that* much older than you. I'm not ancient, you know."

"Yes, ma'am. I mean, no, ma'am, you're not. Ancient, I mean."

He was so nervous he could barely talk. It had been a while since Louise had been around a man this young and innocent, but she remembered how they were. Enough of them had come to the house where she worked, so nervous and so eager at the same time.

She dropped her eyes demurely. "I know an apology won't mean much to you now, but I thought if you'd let me explain. . . ."

Hank swallowed. "Explain what, ma'am? I mean, Louise."

She looked up and met his eyes then, putting an expression of sincere regret on her face. "I'm talking about what happened to you and your grandfather. I'm so sorry about all of it.''

Hank glanced away. "That part of it's over and done with. I'll finish the rest when I catch up to Clayborne."

"I just wanted to tell you that I had no idea what Abner was going to do. I . . . I knew he was a thief, but I didn't know that he was a—a killer, too.''

"He stole that gold, didn't he?" Hank asked grimly.

Louise nodded. "Yes. It was all his idea. He and the others stole it from the Confederate Army at Fort Smith. I didn't know about that, either, until they had already done it and we were on the run. I'm ashamed to say it now, Hank, but it didn't bother me too much that the gold was stolen. You see, I've never had much in my life, and I wanted things to be better. Not just for me, mind you, but for Beth, too. I have her to think of, you know.''

"I reckon I can understand that, all right. I never had a sister, but I can imagine what it's like to have somebody you want to take care of."

"Exactly. Neither Beth nor I have had it easy. I just wanted a better life for both of us.''

"Can't hold that against you," Hank said. It felt good for Louise to be confiding in him this way.

"What . . . what are you going to do with the gold if you get it back from Abner?" She put what she hoped was just the right amount of hope and trembling desperation in her voice.

"Why, I reckon it'll go back to the Confederate government. That's where it came from." Hank suddenly looked thoughtful as the seed planted by Louise began to sprout. "Leastways, I figured I'd return *most* of it. I don't reckon it'd hurt anything if a little of it wound up somewhere else, especially somewhere that it could do some good.''

"I know what you mean, Hank," Louise whispered. She reached out and rested a warm hand on his upper arm. "Thank you.''

She was leaning awfully close to him now, Hank

thought, close enough that he could feel the heat of her leg as it pressed against his. Close enough that he could feel her breath on his cheek as she whispered her gratitude. He looked down at her, blinking and trying to figure out what to do next, when Louise took matters into her own hands.

She reached up and twined her fingers in his hair, pulling his face to hers and opening her lips under his. His arms went around her and drew her tightly against him, so that the lush curves of her body were molded to him.

Hank felt like his head was so light that it was going to jump off his neck and go floating off into the night. The way Louise kissed beat Rose Ellen Hobbs all hollow.

Beth stirred and coughed slightly from her blanket several yards away, and Louise pulled back. She didn't believe that Beth was going to wake up, but she didn't want to chance it. She couldn't take Hank much farther this first time, anyway, without risking his losing control.

There would be other times. When the showdown came, Hank would think first of her and what she wanted.

"Forgive me," she breathed, resting her head against his chest for a moment. "I just want to talk to you, to explain . . . to make some of it up to you somehow. Please don't think I'm too forward."

"Oh, no, ma'am, I don't," Hank exclaimed. "And don't you worry about a thing. I know how rough all this has been on you. I'll take care of you and your sister."

"I knew I could count on you. I knew you were a good man." Let him think she had forgotten how old he really was.

She lifted a hand and stroked his cheek. "Good night, Hank," she whispered, and she managed to put a world of promise in the three words.

On the other side of the ashes, Beth lay on her side and stared into the shadows. Her eyes were wide and dry, though she almost wished that more tears would come. She had heard every word of the conversation between

Louise and Hank, and she had heard that long moment of silence, too. She knew Louise well enough to know what they had been doing then.

Why? Why was Louise leading him on, deceiving him? There were no answers in the night for Beth.

Less than twenty feet away, Buffalo Newcomb crouched behind a mesquite and thought about what he had seen and heard. Unlike Beth, he knew damn well the answer to the question of why Louise was playing up to Hank.

The answer was soft metal, metal that shone so pretty when the light hit it right. . . .

The days seemed to get hotter and longer, but they proceeded. They passed Rattlesnake Spring, and Buffalo only had to kill four of the serpents that gave the place its name. He speared them casually with his knife, pinning them just behind the head with the Arkansas Toothpick, seemingly unafraid. Hank couldn't have done it so nonchalantly. He had a healthy respect for rattlesnakes.

A small range of mountains identified by Buffalo as the Carizos heaved up from the desert floor, but it was no trouble to skirt them. There were more hills and mesas now, though the land was still flat for the most part.

Hank was beginning to worry about their supplies, which were running low, but the day after they had put the Carizo Mountains behind them, they topped a little rise and reined in. Hank, Buffalo, Louise and Beth looked down at a broad, sluggish stream meandering along between shallow banks.

"That there's the Rio," Buffalo said. "Them mountains you can see over younder're in Mexico."

"How far are we from El Paso?"

"Reckon another day or two ridin' up the river will get us there."

"Good. I'm ready to be there."

"I think we all are," Louise said.

Buffalo kneed the mule into motion. As he led the way

down the slope into the river's miles-wide valley, he patted the burlap bag hanging from his saddlehorn. The possum's long, pink, scarred snout poked out one of the holes.

"Headin' back to Mexico, Stink," Buffalo said heartily to the animal. "You recollect all them tortillas you used to eat there? And the time I gave you a jalapeno pepper? Never seen an animal do such a dance as you did that day, ol' hoss!" Buffalo's laugh boomed out while Stink hissed, almost as if he understood the words and remembered.

There were more settlements now that they had reached the river, and the little group was able to replenish its provisions. While they were stopping in one of the villages, Louise and Beth sought out the shade of a cottonwood tree while Hank and Buffalo visited the local store. They could see the women from where they were, in case anyone took them for two helpless females traveling alone.

When they were through in the store and stepped out into the street once again, Buffalo jerked a big thumb at the adobe building next door. "I could use a drink, boy," he rumbled. "You ever tried any o' that Mexican hooch?"

Hank shook his head. "Don't believe I have."

"The ladies look like they're doin' fine right where they are." Buffalo took Hank's arm in a big hand. "Come on, son. I'll tell you all about the worm."

Hank frowned but let Buffalo lead him into the cantina. It commanded a view of the cottonwood tree, too, and Hank knew he could keep an eye on the women from there. He resolved not to let Buffalo stay too long in the place.

Besides, this would give him another opportunity to ask about Clayborne. The man working in the store had said that he hadn't seen any white men in wagons in recent days.

Buffalo strode over to the bar and ordered something

in loud Spanish. Hank lingered near the door. Buffalo brought a bottle and two glasses and steered Hank to a table. As he sat down, the chair groaning beneath his weight, he said, "Reckon we'd best set where we can see them fillies." He pulled the cork from the bottle with his teeth and splashed almost colorless liquid in the glasses. "Here ye go," he said as he pushed one of them over to Hank.

Hank picked up the glass uncertainly. The strong smell of the liquor assaulted his nose, but he tried to ignore it as he lifted the glass to his lips and threw the fiery stuff down his throat.

"Prime stuff, ain't it?" Buffalo asked gleefully as Hank turned red, gagged, and pounded his free hand on the table. He swallowed his own drink with no noticeable effect and poured another for both of them, even though Hank tried to shake his head. "Hell, it's good for what ails ya," Buffalo insisted.

"What ails me is this!" Hank declared, his eyes streaming tears.

When his vision cleared he asked Buffalo, "When do you think we'll reach El Paso?"

"Ought to reach 'er late tomorrow." Buffalo looked at him for a long moment before saying anything. Finally he said, "You're thinkin' them deep thoughts again, ain't you?"

"Just hoping I'm ready for whatever happens up there," Hank replied. "I hope that Clayborne hasn't already gone."

"Luck's bound to be on our side," Buffalo declared. "How could it take a hand against a couple of handsome fellers like us?"

Hank smiled. "I suppose you're right."

"Damn right I'm right. Hell, a younker your age hadn't ought to be thinkin' such gloomy thoughts anyway."

"That's another thing," Hank said. "My age."

"What about it?"

"I got to thinking about it a couple of nights ago,"

Hank said softly. "As best as I can figure it, I turned sixteen four days ago."

"You did? Well, congratulations, son, late or not."

"That's just it. I never even thought about it being my birthday. I forgot all about it. Before I couldn't wait to turn sixteen and become a man."

"Reckon that happened anyway, son."

Buffalo tossed off his second drink and said, "You'd better keep up, boy, else you'll be left with the worm."

"What worm?"

Buffalo lifted the bottle and tilted it so that Hank could see . . . something . . . in the bottom of it. "That there's a worm, boy," Buffalo said. "Man that finishes off the bottle gets to eat 'im." He smacked his lips.

Hank swallowed and pushed his glass away, the second drink untouched. "It's all yours," he said weakly. "I wouldn't want to deprive you."

"Reckon that's up to you," Buffalo grinned. "If you ain't drinkin' anymore, no use bein' polite, is there?" He picked up the bottle and drank directly from the neck, the *pulque* gurgling as he swallowed.

Hank supposed that everyone had his own way of killing himself. Standing up, he glanced at the women and walked over to the bar. There were a few men drinking there, a mixture of Mexicans and Texans, but the bartender wasn't busy. He came over to Hank and said, "Can I help you?"

"I just want to ask you a question."

The man shrugged his shoulders. "I am a humble man and know little, but I will answer if I can."

"Have you seen anything of four white men traveling through here in the last few days, driving a couple of wagons?"

"Another man, he asked the same question," the bartender said. "Only he said the men had two señoritas with them."

Hank put his hands on the bar. "Somebody else was looking for the same men?"

"*Sí*, a gringo like yourself, a tall man."

Hank shook his head. This was just too much to figure out. "Had you seen the men he was looking for?"

"No, señor. I told him this also."

Hank leaned on the bar and tried to make some sense of it. It sure sounded like somebody else was after Clayborne. Maybe it was the man Doc Yantis told him about.

Hopefully it would all straighten itself out when they got to El Paso. For the moment, all Hank hoped was that nobody else caught up to Clayborne before him.

He wanted the pleasure of that moment all to himself.

He turned back to the table and saw Buffalo Newcomb licking his lips with great relish. The *pulque* bottle sat in the center of the table, empty.

═══ *Seventeen* ═══

The streets were quite busy as Enos strolled across Stanton, even though the hour was getting late. He kept his eyes open for trouble, but no one had bothered him since his arrival in El Paso.

A bartender had suggested asking at Espinoza's undertaking establishment if he was looking for information about anything going on in El Paso. He found it without any trouble, simply by walking down Stanton Street toward the river. The place was dark and locked up, though, and no one responded to Enos's knock on the door. As he stood in front of the building, he looked south, toward the river, and thought about whether or not he wanted to go over into Mexico tonight. The idea didn't appeal to him, but Espinoza was the only real lead he had. He didn't want to waste any more time, and Espinoza was supposed to be the best informed man in the area.

He turned his steps toward the Rio Grande and the wooden bridge spanning it. Before he had gone a block, something stopped him. A voice came floating through the night air, a sweet voice accompanied by the gentle strumming of a guitar. He had heard it before, in a little cantina downriver. Just before the killing started.

He told himself to ignore it, that it was just coincidence and had nothing to do with him. But something about the tones drew him on, down a side street to another little cantina much like the other one. This one had a small patio to one side with a few tables scattered on a flagstone pavement. The girl was singing there, to a small audience.

A short rock wall ran around the patio. Enos stepped over it and went to an empty table. A waiter came up to him a moment later and took his order for a beer. Enos gave the order in a low voice, not wanting to interfere with the girl's song.

She looked much the same tonight, wearing the same red gown and comb in her hair. And the songs she sang were the same as well. Her voice still throbbed with passion, and Enos found himself so carried along with the music that he barely noticed when the waiter returned with his beer.

There were several cottonwoods around the patio, and it was lit by lamps hanging in their branches. The illumination gave the place a soft glow, and Enos wasn't surprised that most of the tables were occupied by couples.

The girl brought her song to a close and waited for a moment while several of the couples politely applauded. Then the *vaquero* with the guitar launched into another tune and she began to sing again.

This was the kind of place she belonged in, Enos thought. The little cantina downriver was rough and rowdy, and the customers there showed no appreciation of the girl's special talents.

Enos wondered why he was paying so much attention to her himself. She was attractive, no doubt about that, but he didn't think that was the reason. He liked a pretty girl as much as the next man, but romance was the farthest thing from his mind right now. He was here on a job for the State of Texas, and that was all that mattered.

He lifted the mug of beer halfway to his lips and suddenly stopped there. The girl had turned her head so that she could see him better, and her eyes met his with an intensity that was like a physical jolt down Enos's spine.

What the hell . . . ?

There was no explanation for it, but it was like she was reaching out to him, imploring him to do . . . *something*. He put the beer back on the table, untouched.

Her voice never faltered, and after a moment she was able to move her gaze away from him as she finished the song. But when she was done, she turned abruptly and went into the cantina almost at a run. The guitar player looked after her in puzzlement, then thanked the audience in Spanish and went into the cantina, too.

Enos stared at the table for long moments, trying to make some sense of what had happened here tonight. There was no answer, though. As far as he knew, the girl had no connection with him except for being in the same village the night he had killed Pablo Garzón.

There was no figuring it out unless he could find out more, and he didn't have time for that. He should have already been across the river, looking for Espinoza. He stood up and left money on the table to pay for the beer he hadn't drank, then left the patio and headed back toward Stanton Street.

He had gone half a block when a figure launched itself out of a shadowy alley. Moonlight flickered on the blade of a knife coming directly at Enos's heart.

Instinct taking over, he twisted to the side and let the attacker slide past him. He drove an elbow out and felt it thump into the man's side, staggering him. Enos kept turning, deftly sliding his Colt from its holster and lashing out with it. The barrel cracked into the knife wielder's skull and pitched him forward on his face.

The pad of feet on hard-packed dirt and the rustle of cloth warned Enos. He went to one knee, ducking as another knife ripped through the air where his head had been a second before. A bulky body crashed into him and knocked him off balance. He went down, the second attacker falling on top of him.

Enos reached out and closed the fingers of his left hand over the man's wrist. He strained to hold the blade away from his face as he tried to get the gun in position. Ramming the barrel into the man's side, Enos squeezed the trigger.

The man's body muffled the explosion of the shot, but the blast threw him to the side, the knife clattering away in the darkness. He screamed and gurgled and then lay still as Enos scrambled to his feet.

There were more of them, coming out of every alleyway. He could see them as fleeting shapes, darker patches of shadow that darted toward him. There were four bullets left in his gun, and he triggered them off in one rolling wave of fire as he spun around. He couldn't tell if any of them hit anything, but the closing circle around him hesitated and then broke for a second.

Enos summoned up all the speed he possessed, trusting his luck that he wouldn't run into anything in the dark. He didn't like to run from a fight, but the odds were just too great. He would have been cut to ribbons if he had tried to stand up to them.

Behind him, he could hear yelling now. He heard Pablo Garzón's name being shouted and knew that his past was catching up to him. His hopes of being left alone to handle his investigation were gone.

Orange bursts of gunfire blossomed in the darkness behind him. The streets were dimly lit and he was a running target. It would take an awfully lucky shot to hit him.

A big hand slapped his hip, knocking him off stride and sending him sprawling in the filthy street.

He came up running again, and somehow he had held on to his gun during the spill. But there was a burning pain in his hip, and he could feel a warm, wet sensation on his right thigh. Every step made the pain worse, but he couldn't stop, not with a mob behind him, howling for his blood. He didn't know where he was now. The streets all looked alike at night, even when you weren't running for your life. But he saw a door open up ahead and to his left, saw the light of a lamp spill through the opening for an instant before it was extinguished. He lifted the Colt, ready to fire if anyone got in his way.

"Wait!"

The command was hissed in a low voice, but even so Enos recognized it. He hesitated, slowing down, and a hand came out of the darkness and urged him toward the door. He had a fleeting glimpse of long, raven hair and dark eyes that looked deeply into his.

Then he was inside the building and the door was being shut softly behind him, leaving him in utter blackness.

The wound on his hip was little more than a crease, but it had bled quite a bit and left his right leg stiff. It also hurt like the very devil when the girl cleaned it out with whiskey. Enos bit his lip and didn't cry out as she worked with her soft, deft hands, cleansing the wound and then tying a clean piece of cloth over it for a bandage.

Her name was Elena María Rodríguez, and she and her brother Jorge were staying in the narrow little house where she had brought him. She had talked quite a bit once the bloodthirsty mob hunting Enos had passed by, but until then the two of them had stood without moving, almost without breathing, in the darkness. Enos hadn't had the slightest damn notion what he had gotten into, but anything was better than being ripped to pieces by a bunch of killers.

When they were gone, she had lit a candle and bent to examine the wound. She grimaced and sharply sucked in her breath when she saw the spreading bloodstain on his pants leg, but her face and voice were determined as she told him, "The pants. Take them down."

"Nothing but a scratch, ma'am," Enos insisted,

though he hadn't known that was true at the time. "I can take care of it."

"I have many brothers, señor," she had insisted dryly. "A man bleeding like a pig should not be so modest . . . or so stubborn."

The wound was throbbing, and Enos was light-headed enough that he knew he was feeling the blood loss. He just didn't have the strength to argue with her. He slid his pants down just enough so that she could get to the wound, and one of his hands was never far from the butt of the Walker Colt.

While she worked, he said, "Considerin' the circumstances, I reckon we ought to introduce ourselves. I'm Enos Littleton."

"Elena María Rodríguez," she said without looking up.

"Why did you help me? And what was the look about that you gave me back at the cantina?"

"You are the man who killed Pablo Garzón. That means I owe you a debt that I can never repay." Her voice was low, intense. Still she did not look up at him.

"You have a grudge against Garzón?" Enos asked, determined to get to the bottom of this.

"I have wished for four years to see him dead."

Enos waited silently, hoping she would go on. A few moments later, she did.

"You have seen the one who plays the guitar while I sing," she said. It was a statement, not a question. "That is my brother Jorge. When I left the cantina, I told him to stay if he wished. That is why he is not here. One of my other brothers was named Lindo. But he is dead."

"What happened?" Enos asked when she paused again. He felt a little bit like he was prying, but she seemed to want to tell him about this.

"He was killed trying to hold up one of the Butterfield stagecoaches, back when they were still running. He was with Pablo Garzón at the time."

"And you blame Garzón for your brother's death?"

Enos drew in a sharp hissing breath as she splashed whiskey into the wound.

"Who would you have me blame? The guard who was only doing what he is paid to do? Or the man who was really responsible for Lindo even being there? I chose to hate Garzón. That is why I began singing in the cantinas along the river. I knew that sooner or later I would get a chance to have my revenge on Garzón. He came into all of those places; it was just a matter of time. But the night I finally found him, you were there, too."

"And I cheated you out of your revenge, is that it?"

"I did not care who killed him. He was a dog and should have been shot long ago." She tied the bandage on his hip, her gentle touch at odds with the savage words. "Fate permitted me to see him die. That was enough."

Enos pulled up his pants, then gestured around at the dimly lit room. "Then why all of this?" He was talking not only about the room, but about the way she had rescued him from the mob.

"As I said, I owe you a debt. This was the beginning of its repayment." She straightened and tilted her face up so that she could look into his eyes.

He reached up and cupped her chin, lifting her head so that she was ready when he kissed her. Her lips were warm and moist and inviting as all hell, and Enos had more trouble than he had expected pulling away from her.

"I'd say we're even now," he rasped, his voice thick with emotion.

"No, never. . . ."

"Yes," he insisted. "Listen, Elena, I came to El Paso hunting some men, and when I find them, there'll probably be some shooting. And Garzón's people are after me. It's better if you just go on with your life and forget about me."

"I cannot do that. I—"

The sudden opening of the door made both of them

jerk around. Enos's hand flew to his Colt, and he had it halfway out of the holster when Elena cried, "Jorge!"

The *vaquero* from the cantina stood there, without his guitar now. He was swaying slightly, just enough to show that he had been drinking. He saw how close Elena and Enos were standing. Jorge Rodríguez turned his head and spat.

"*Puta!* This is why you had to come to El Paso? To see the gringo who killed one of Mexico's greatest men?"

"Pablo Garzón was not a man!" Elena blazed at her brother, taking a step toward him. "He was a miserable worm who was responsible for Lindo's death! Have you forgotten?"

"Lindo was a fool who should have shot that bastard of a guard when he had a chance! It was not Pablo's fault."

Elena threw her hands up. "Ah! You are impossible!"

Jorge reached out and put one hand on the edge of the doorway to steady himself. He started cursing her in low, stinging Spanish, until Enos stepped forward and grated, "You've got no call to talk to your sister like that, amigo. You'd best leave it alone."

"I am not afraid of you, gringo!" Jorge snapped. His hand suddenly darted inside his short jacket. "I will kill you myself!"

Enos saw the little pepperbox pistol in Jorge's hand as it emerged from under the jacket. He could have drawn and fired, but he didn't want to risk a shot. Not to mention the fact that he didn't want to kill Elena's brother.

He took a quick step forward, ignoring the twinge of pain in his hip, and reached out with his left hand. His fingers caught Jorge's wrist and twisted it roughly. At the same time, he brought his right fist across in a short punch that cracked against the Mexican's jaw.

The pepperbox flew out of Jorge's hand and went skittering away. His head snapped around from the blow, and his legs seemed to turn to rubber. Enos let go of his wrist, and Jorge sat down heavily in the dirt.

He was only down for a moment, though, and then he came to his feet, looking around desperately for the fallen gun. Enos slipped his Colt from its holster. "Forget it, boy."

Jorge cast a wild-eyed glance at him, then abruptly turned and began to run down the street. He vanished into the shadows in a matter of seconds.

Elena put a hand on Enos's arm as he holstered the Colt. "I am sorry," she said. "My brother, he does not understand many things. . . ."

"It's all right," Enos told her. He put his hands on her shoulders. "I've got to be going now."

"I wish . . ." Elena began, and then her voice trailed off, unsure of what she wanted to say next.

After a moment, Enos said, "I do, too."

And then he was gone, striding away into the night, back on the trail of the men he was seeking.

Eighteen

Abner Clayborne rasped a hand over his unshaven jaw and watched the sun come up. The stubble on his face bothered him, as did the fact that he hadn't bathed in several days. He had always been fastidious in his personal habits.

The long night was over, and though he hated to leave the gold, he knew he had to get out of this smelly livery barn. Reed and Smith could be trusted to stand guard over the coffin.

Ordway slouched up to stand in the double doors next to Clayborne. "We headin' for the hotel?" he asked.

"As soon as Reuben and Smith get here," Clayborne said.

"Be glad to get some shut-eye. It's been a hard trip. It'd be all right with me if it took a few days to set things up again."

Clayborne gave him a hard look. "The longer we stay in El Paso, the more chance that someone will catch us."

"Who?" Ordway asked with a savage grin. "Kimbell? Let him come. I can handle him."

"I'm sure you can, Gus. But I'd prefer that we not have to find out."

Clayborne looked down the street toward the hotel and saw Reed and Smith emerge from the lobby onto the porch. As they approached, he could see that both of them looked a bit haggard. The hour was early, and all of them had been drained by the past few weeks, just as Ordway had said.

"Morning," Reed said as they came into the barn. He looked past Clayborne and Ordway to where Jiménez was bringing water to the horses stabled there. "Any trouble?"

"None at all," Clayborne replied. He clapped Reed on the shoulder. "We're going to leave you and Bob here, Reuben. Don't let anyone near that coffin."

"Don't you worry about a thing, Abner," Reed assured him. "Anybody who tries to touch it is a dead man."

Clayborne nodded and stepped out into the street, turning toward the hotel. Ordway walked behind him. They had only gone a few feet when a carriage pulled up to them.

"Ah, Señor Clayborne!" Espinoza exclaimed from the seat of the carriage. "I hoped that I would be able to find you. I have good luck to report." The Mexican undertaker's lean face was even more gaunt than before, indicating that he had been up all night.

"You've located Garzón?" Clayborne asked.

"I have discovered what happened to him. He was killed several nights ago in a village downriver from here. I do not know all the details, but I was told that he was shot by a tall gringo in a cantina. His people have trailed the man here to El Paso and are even now looking for him in order to exact their revenge." Espinoza waved a hand. "But that does not concern us. What is important is that I have arranged for you to proceed with safety into Mexico."

Clayborne drew a deep breath of satisfaction. "Excellent. What do we do now?"

"Rest. Tonight, we will take your wagon across the river and meet the men who will escort you on your destination."

"These men. They are trustworthy, I take it?"

Espinoza nodded. "The very best. You do not need to worry, señor."

"All right." Clayborne wasn't sure whether or not he believed Espinoza about the trustworthiness of the men he had hired, but some chances had to be taken. He was confident in his own abilities and those of his companions. They could handle any trouble that came their way.

For the time being, all he really wanted was a bath, followed by some sleep and perhaps even a shave.

Clayborne lifted a hand briefly in farewell as Espinoza drove away in the carriage. Ordway stood next to him, hands on his hips, and said, "I don't know about trustin' that greaser overmuch, boss."

"I don't trust anyone overmuch, Gus," Clayborne said with a faint smile.

Thaddeus Kimbell woke from sleep like he was drugged. His eyes didn't want to open, and his head was pounding. But he forced himself to sit up and look around the room.

He was in a bed with a lumpy mattress, the only piece of furniture in a narrow hotel room where the wallpaper was peeling from the walls. The place was squalid, but it was cheap.

After days of traveling, he had arrived in El Paso almost out of money with his spirits sagging. And Louise's betrayal was always with him.

He was able to dress and leave the hotel and eat breakfast at a small cafe. Then he reclaimed his horse from the livery barn behind the hotel and rode toward downtown. He had to get back to his mission, his sacred mission of revenge.

The day was beautiful, with bright sunshine washing down over the river and the city nestled between mountains. A cool breeze blew out of the west, relieving the heat. Kimbell glanced up at Mount Franklin, reminded for a moment of the Ozarks, although this peak was much rockier and lacked the abundant vegetation of the mountains in Arkansas.

He asked everyone who gave him a chance about Clayborne and the others, but no one would admit seeing them. Frustration built in him as the day went by with no more success than all the previous days.

Perhaps he had been underestimating Clayborne. Perhaps he and the gold were already in Mexico, getting farther away with every passing hour. Kimbell knew he couldn't linger too long here in El Paso.

But if finding Clayborne in Texas had been a difficult job, locating him in the wilds of Mexico would be almost too impossible to contemplate.

Kimbell sighed, pausing in the dusty street to remove his hat and wipe the sweat from its band. He glanced at the big barn he was standing in front of. It was a livery stable, he saw from the sign above the doors, owned by a man named Jiménez. One of the doors was open, and Kimbell glanced into the shadowy interior.

There were wagons parked there. . . .

Kimbell suddenly stiffened, his eyes narrowing. *Wagons*. He stepped to the doorway, setting his hat back on his head so that both hands were free. His fingers hovered near the butt of his army Colt.

There was a Conestoga wagon, and parked beside it a buckboard with something in the back. Kimbell squinted, trying to make out what it was. Could it be a coffin?

Was Clayborne already dead? No, it couldn't be! He couldn't be cheated out of his revenge like that!

Drawing his pistol, he pushed the door all the way open and stepped inside. His eyes had adjusted by now, and he could see a thick-waisted Mexican carrying a sack of grain. The man stopped in his tracks and dropped the sack when he saw Kimbell standing there with a gun.

"Anyone else here?" Kimbell asked harshly.

The Mexican shook his head. "No, señor," he said, his voice shaking. "Jus' me."

Kimbell gestured at the wagons with his free hand, keeping the Colt pointed in the man's general direction. "Who owns those wagons?" he demanded.

"Those wagons? They belong to Señor Espinoza, the *embalsamador*. The undertaker, señor."

Kimbell felt his hopes fall. He sighed heavily. So that was a coffin, and there was probably a very good reason for it being there. As for the Conestoga, there were plenty of them in the West. Not all of them belonged to Abner Clayborne.

"All right," Kimbell said. He holstered the gun. "I'm sorry I bothered you."

The Mexican waved his hands. *"De nada, de nada. Buenos días, señor."*

Kimbell walked out of the barn, dejected. Another hope dashed. And this time he had felt so close. His gut had been screaming at him that he had finally found Clayborne.

"Damn," Reuben Reed breathed, crouching in one of the stalls. Bob Smith was close beside him, gun out and ready. "I thought Kimbell had us for sure that time," Reed went on.

"I should've just dropped him and got it over with," Smith said. He rammed his pistol back in its holster.

"That would have drawn attention to us, and Clayborne doesn't want that."

Reed stepped out and nodded to the Mexican, who was picking up the sack he had dropped. "Good job, Jiménez. Looked like you convinced him."

"Sí. But you told me what to say, señor."

It had taken some quick thinking, all right, once Reed spotted Kimbell just outside the stable. He had hoped that Kimbell would just go on and not notice the wagons, but some rapidly whispered instructions to Jiménez had taken care of the situation.

Kimbell might come back, though. The man was like a leech. Reed wasn't convinced that they had shaken him, wouldn't be convinced until they had a lot of miles of Mexican soil behind them.

He pulled his watch from his pocket and glanced at the face. "Four o'clock," he told Smith. "Clayborne ought to be awake again by now. I'm going to the hotel to tell him that Kimbell is here."

"All right by me," Smith replied.

"You and that coffin better be here when I get back."

Smith grinned. "If I was goin' to steal it, I'd a done it a long time before now, Reed."

Reed nodded and went to the door, checking to see if Kimbell was anywhere in sight. Satisfied that it was safe, he hurried out and down the street to the hotel.

He found Abner Clayborne shaving in front of the mirror in his room. Clayborne looked rested and relaxed, and the cruel light that sometimes shone in his eyes was nowhere to be seen. He looked friendly and prosperous, like a banker.

"Trouble, Abner," Reed announced as soon as he came into the room. "Kimbell's here."

Clayborne's face tightened, but he didn't lose his smile. "I expected that," he said. "The man should just give up, but I fear he won't. Well, we'll just have to deal with him if he tries to interfere with us."

"He came into the stable and saw the wagons, nearly caught Smith and me. The Mexican convinced him that the wagons belong to Espinoza, though."

Clayborne nodded. "Very good. I'm expecting Espinoza at any moment, to let me know exactly when we'll be crossing the bridge into Mexico."

"Can't be any too soon for me," Reed said vehemently.

Ordway came into the room from the hall, just back

from a visit to the outhouse behind the hotel. Clayborne told him what was happening and sent him to the stable to stand guard with Smith and to tell Jiménez to close up. Ordway checked the loads in his gun. "I hope Kimbell does come back. It'd be a pleasure to kill that son of a bitch."

Espinoza arrived ten minutes later, also looking much fresher than he had that morning. Clayborne poured him a drink from a bottle of whiskey on the dresser.

Espinoza smacked his lips over the liquor, then said, "Can you be ready to leave at ten tonight, señor?"

"Definitely," Clayborne replied.

"Then if you will come to the bridge at the end of Stanton Street, I will meet you there and escort you over. The others will be waiting for us across the river."

"It sounds like an excellent arrangement. You'll receive your fee when we're safely on the other side."

Espinoza nodded and finished off the drink. *"Bueno.* It has been a pleasure doing business with you, señor."

He didn't offer to shake hands before he left, and Clayborne was glad of that. Bad enough the man was Mexican, but he was an undertaker as well.

Now all that was left to do was wait until ten o'clock.

"Well, Reuben," Clayborne said, slapping the other man on the shoulder, "shall we go downstairs and see what sort of repast this establishment's dining room has to offer?"

Enos had found an out-of-the-way rooming house the night before and spent an uneasy few hours tossing and turning in a hard bed. He kept his Colt in his hand the whole time. Finally, toward dawn, he had dropped off for a couple of hours, but as the sun rose, he awoke with a new sense of urgency gripping him.

Something about this day was going to be different. He could feel it in his bones. And years of living on the frontier had taught him to trust his instincts.

He wasn't going to sit in a little room and hide out just

because somebody was hunting him. There was a job waiting to be done. He got up and started trying to do it.

He spent the day talking to bartenders and storekeepers and anyone else he could find. Most of the time, people just shrugged when he questioned them and said, "Sorry, mister, can't help you." A few times he was told that he was the second man to ask that question. And at least a dozen times, he cussed the way folks went about their own business and didn't pay that much attention to what else went on around them. That was just human nature, and there wasn't a damn thing you could do to change it.

It wasn't until nearly dusk that he talked to a whiskered old-timer who pulled on his beard and said, "Seems to me I seen some wagons come into town yestiddy evenin'."

"Did you see where they went?"

The old man shrugged. "Don't rightly believe I did. But was I you, I'd check down to Jiménez's livery."

Enos thought back to the places he had been today and said with a frown, "I went by there earlier. The place was all locked up, had a closed sign on the door. I reckoned the owner was either sick or out of business."

The old-timer shook his head. "Don't think so. Sure ain't like that Meskin to be closed."

Enos felt a prickling along his spine. This old man might have just given him the lead he needed. He just hoped it turned out better than the last one. He had thought that Espinoza might be able to tell him about the men he was looking for, but the undertaker seemed to have dropped off the face of the earth.

"Thanks," Enos told the old man. "Reckon I'll go on down there and take another look."

As he walked toward the livery stable, the sun slid out of sight to the west. Night would fall quickly now, and lights were starting to be lit all over town.

Enos saw the stable up ahead. The double doors were still closed, and he could see the same sign nailed to one of them. According to the old man, that was a strange enough occurrence to warrant checking out.

His eyes strayed to the other end of the street. All day, there had been quite a bit of traffic, but it had hit a lull right now. A lot of people were eating their supper. Four riders were coming into town, their horses ambling down the middle of the street at an easy pace. They were too far away for Enos to distinguish anything about them except for the fact that one of them was a pretty good-sized old boy. He looked back at the stable, already forgetting the four strangers.

When he was still half the distance from the stable, all hell broke loose.

"There he is!" someone yelled, and the voice was too damned familiar. Enos spun, grabbing for his gun.

The scene seemed to freeze for a second in the dusk. Jorge Rodríguez was standing about thirty feet away, a rifle in his hands. There were five men with him, and all were heavily armed. Garzón's *compadres*, Enos knew. Jorge must have been following him, must have led them to him.

The young man snapped the rifle to his shoulder, eager to kill the gringo and make a name for himself as the man who avenged Pablo Garzón.

Enos grimaced. Elena was going to have someone else to cry over. He shot Jorge in the chest.

Jorge went flying back into the other men, slowing them down for a moment as they charged. The rifle fell unfired from his hands as he died. One of the men roughly shoved his body aside and leaped past him, already forgetting him.

Enos ducked into an alley as slugs began to whine around his head. The street suddenly sounded like a war as the men started firing their rifles and revolvers. Splinters stung Enos's face as bullets chewed up the wall beside him.

There was a barrel up ahead on one side of the alley, probably used to collect water during the infrequent rains. Enos toppled it and then threw himself down behind it. Not much cover, but it was the best he could do. The five men scattered as he emptied his Colt at them.

Desperately, he grabbed cartridges from the loops on his shell belt and started reloading. Bullets plunked into the barrel. Some of them were stopped or deflected, but others punched on through. It would only be a matter of seconds before one of them found him. . . .

A giant silhouette on horseback suddenly loomed at the mouth of the alley. What sounded like the roar of a grizzly bear boomed and echoed from wall to wall. The deafening blast of a Sharps rifle assaulted Enos's ears.

The slug from the Sharps caught one of the Mexicans at the breastbone and punched him back against a wall. He bounced off and fell limply, a huge hole in his chest. One of the other men started to whirl around just in time to take the blade of an Arkansas Toothpick across the throat. He tried to scream, but no sound came out with the fountain of blood.

Enos saw what was happening over the top of the barrel, but he could hardly credit his senses. A massive, bearded man drove his horse—no, it was a mule—into one of the remaining Mexicans, trampling the man. Then the giant was leaping off the mule's back and wrapping his long arms around the last man, squeezing until the man's cries were cut off in a pitiful gurgle.

Something prodded at Enos's brain. His rescuer had taken care of four of the men. What had happened to the fifth one? Maybe in the confusion, Enos thought, he had miscounted. Maybe only four men had come down the alley.

But he was sure there had been five men with Jorge—

The scrape of a heel behind him was the only warning he had. Enos went to one side in a dive as a gun blasted. He landed heavily, and the Colt slipped from his fingers. He looked up, saw the Mexican standing there ready to fire the final shot.

There was a sharp crack that sounded like a Henry rifle, and the man's head jerked backward. He flopped crazily, shot clean between the eyes.

"Hell of a shot, younker," came a rumbling voice. That had to be the big bearded man. Enos picked up his Colt and swung to face him. The blood was still pounding in his head. He'd looked death in the face a time or two before, but it didn't get any easier.

Someone else was standing beside the big man, someone tall and broad-shouldered and holding a Henry rifle. He reached up and cuffed back his hat, revealing a shock of blond hair and a lean, youthful face.

Enos suddenly felt like it was he who had gotten shot between the eyes.

"Hello, Pa," Hank said.

Nineteen

Hank still felt like somebody had yanked the world out from under him and put it back wrong. When he and Buffalo and the two women had ridden into town, they had heard the gunfire break out. Buffalo had growled, "Five against one. Don't like them odds, boy."

But Hank had been busy staring at the lone man being attacked. He had had only a glimpse of him before he ducked out of sight, but that one look was enough.

"That's my pa!" he had yelled.

Buffalo spurred the mule into a gallop and threw himself into the fight, while Hank fought off the shock of seeing his father long enough to down the last of the attackers. The long shot in the shadowy alley had been purely an instinctive thing. There hadn't been time to aim, or even light enough, for that matter.

They stood on the sidewalk facing each other, and Hank knew that Enos was thinking the same thing. The two of them were strangers, bound by blood maybe, but not much else. A few scattered memories of good times, like that day they had gone fishing. . . .

"Grandpa's dead," Hank said. He knew it was a hard way of telling Enos, but he didn't know what else to say.

A muscle twitched in Enos's cheek. "What happened?"

Before Hank could answer, Buffalo stepped up and said, "Reckon I'll take these little ladies over to the hotel and get 'em settled in. You and your pa can talk private like that way." He gestured with a massive hand at the del Norte across the street. "Meet ya over yonder at that waterin' hole later."

"All right," Hank nodded. He didn't much like the idea of talking to Enos alone, but he supposed Buffalo was right. They had things to say to each other.

Buffalo ushered Louise and Beth down the street to the hotel. Hank watched them go into the building, then turned back to Enos. "Reckon you'll be shocked, Pa, if I offer to buy you a drink?"

"Not so shocked that I won't take you up on it."

Enos was having a hard time accepting this strapping young man as his son. Hank had sure as hell changed since he had seen the boy last. Boy? Hank was a man now.

They started to walk together across the street, but when they were halfway to the saloon, a heavyset, middle-aged man wearing a sheriff's star hurried up to them. "Hold on there, you two," he said sharply. "Folks told me you was involved in that shootin' a little while ago."

"Reckon I was the cause of it, Sheriff," Enos said wearily. "It was me that the dead men were after. Name's Enos Littleton."

The sheriff squinted shrewdly at him. "I just took a gander at the bodies. They was Pablo Garzón's men, and I've been hearin' a rumor that somebody shot Garzón downriver. You know anything about that?"

"Afraid I do. It was me that shot him, but I didn't have a whole lot of choice." Enos dropped his voice lower, so that no one but Hank and the sheriff could hear him. "I'm a Texas Ranger, here on assignment."

The sheriff frowned. "A Ranger, huh? Got any proof of that?"

Enos shook his head. "No, sir, I don't. Nothing except my word."

After a long moment, the lawman said, "I've knowed a few Rangers in my time. Reckon your word's good enough for me, son. There's just one thing. . . . You ain't plannin' on stayin' in El Paso long, are you?"

Enos couldn't help but smile a little. "I hope not, Sheriff. I want to finish this job and go home."

"You do that." The sheriff walked away to tend to the bodies of the dead Mexicans.

Hank and Enos went on into the del Norte and found a table that wasn't occupied. Enos's voice and face became grim. "Now tell me what happened."

Hank told him, covering the story quickly but not leaving out any of the details. He explained about the special coffin, the lie about Reed and Ordway being Confederate agents, the way he and Thomas had been shot down. Trenches appeared in Enos's cheeks as he listened.

He didn't say anything until after Hank had told about meeting Buffalo Newcomb and the encounter with Louise and Beth Shelby. Hank could tell that his father was very surprised by what he had heard, but he didn't know just how surprised.

Finally, when Hank fell silent, his mouth dry from talking, Enos said, "They say there's no such thing as coincidence, but I'll be damned if that's not what this is. You trail this Clayborne out here for revenge, son, but I've been trailin' the same bunch as a job for the Rangers."

The del Norte was busy tonight, and a waiter was just now getting to the table to take their order. Enos glanced at Hank and asked, "You drink beer now?"

Hank nodded.

"Two beers," Enos said to the waiter. After the man

was gone, Enos went on, "You're sure you're all right, Hank? Those wounds you got healed up?"

"Buffalo took good care of me," Hank said.

"Well, soon's we get a chance, I'd like to have a doctor take a look at them and—"

"I can take care of myself, Pa," Hank cut in sharply. "I've been doing it for a while now."

Enos looked at him, but Hank wouldn't meet his eyes. "What've you got your back up about, son?" Enos asked.

"Nothing. Just nothing at all. Just . . ." Hank's voice broke slightly. "Maybe if you'd been home, it wouldn't have happened. Maybe Grandpa would be alive."

There was pain in Enos's eyes as he said, "I don't blame you for not understandin', son. Maybe when you're older you will. But I'll tell you this: your grandpa never held it against me that I did what I did. And I knew he'd raise you right." He looked proudly at Hank. "Reckon he did all right."

Hank was glad the waiter arrived with their beers just then. He couldn't think of anything to say to his father except what he had already said. Picking up the mug, he drank deeply. It still didn't taste very good to him, but he didn't want to look like a kid in front of Enos.

The batwings were pushed back by a massive arm, and Buffalo came through them into the saloon, holding the possum in his other hand and letting the animal dangle by its tail. Stink was hissing and looking furious, as usual. Buffalo went to the bar, ignoring the startled looks and the laughter that the possum drew from the other customers.

He lifted Stink onto the bar, setting him down right in front of a stunned bartender. "Look here, mister," the man finally said when he got his voice back, "you can't put that . . . that varmint up on the bar."

Buffalo frowned ferociously and put his other hand on the hilt of his knife. "You sure about that, amigo?"

"Well, I . . . ah . . . Hell, if it don't bother anybody else, it don't bother me."

"Good attitude to have," Buffalo nodded. He spotted the free-lunch tray a few feet away down the bar and reached over to snag a hard-boiled egg from it. "Here yuh go, feller," he said, offering the egg to the possum.

Stink sniffed the egg for a second, then lunged forward and snatched it out of Buffalo's fingers, crunching shell and all as he eagerly ate it.

Enos watched from the table with a smile playing around his lips. "That Buffalo seems like quite a character," he said. "Never did thank him for pitchin' in and helpin' me."

"He'll write a song about it," Hank said. "He writes a song about damn near everything he does."

"You like him a lot, don't you?"

Hank glanced at Enos and said, "He saved my life. He says I saved his, too, but I'm not sure about that. I think he could have handled those Apaches without my help. But I know for sure he saved mine. He was right there when I needed somebody."

Enos bit back the angry retort that he felt coming on. Was the boy ever going to stop comparing and blaming?

Hank knew he wasn't being fair, but as much as he regretted it, he also couldn't help it. There were years of hurt and resentment inside him, and his feelings were forcing their way out since seeing his father again.

Buffalo spotted them sitting at the table and brought Stink and a huge mug of beer with him as he came over to join them.

"Get the girls settled in the hotel all right?" Hank asked as Buffalo pulled out one of the chairs and sat down, the wood of the chair creaking under his weight.

"Got 'em a nice room. That desk clerk was actin' like he sort of smelled somethin' bad, but his tune changed fast enough when I showed him some *dinero*."

Enos sipped his beer and said, "That Clayborne must

be lower'n a snake to abandon two girls out in the middle of nowhere like that.''

"Louise wants to catch up to Clayborne as bad as we do," Hank said. He looked intently at his father and then asked the question that both of them had been thinking. "What happens now? Do we go after Clayborne together? I'm sure as hell not going home until this is finished.''

Enos sighed. It was a question for which he didn't have an answer. A sudden blast of gunfire from somewhere outside saved him the trouble of coming up with one.

Soon, Abner Clayborne thought. Soon they would be in Mexico, on their way to a new life. He wondered how difficult it would be getting slaves in Mexico. They would be brown instead of black, but that didn't matter as long as they worked hard and didn't get uppity.

He pulled back the curtain on the hotel room window and looked outside at the busy street. Then he pulled his watch from its pocket and checked the time. Nine-thirty. In only a half-hour, they would meet Espinoza at the Rio Grande bridge and be on their way.

Reuben Reed snapped shut the valise lying on the bed. "All packed, Abner," he said cheerfully. "Hard to believe we've finally made it this far. Seems like such a long time ago when we left Atlanta.''

"It was a long time ago," Clayborne said, picking up his hat from the dresser. "And a great many things have happened since then.''

His mind went back to the chaos at Atlanta, the town caught in a war frenzy with a growing edge of desperation as things went badly for the South. He had been exceedingly happy to get out of there. The trip to Fort Smith had been arduous, but they had survived. And then the stunning success of their theft of the gold. Louise had been happy.

Louise....

Clayborne knew that he had done the right thing when

he left her on the plains. She had grown extremely tiresome. Beth, now—leaving Beth behind was a pity. Her innocence would have made her exciting in his bed. She would have resisted, but that would have just made it better, more sweet when finally he conquered her.

He shook his head to clear it of such disturbing thoughts. There were much more important things to think about now. He turned to Reed with a smile and said, "Well, shall we go?"

Somewhere downstairs, a woman screamed.

Clayborne's head jerked up. Reed muttered, "What the hell?"

Clayborne's breath seemed lodged in his throat. Grim lines etched themselves on his face. He jerked the door of the room open and snapped, "Hurry, Reuben!"

"But what—"

"Dammit, man! I know that voice!"

In a room on the second floor of the hotel, Beth Shelby sank down on the frilly coverlet of the bed and sighed. "Civilization," she breathed.

Louise smiled slightly. She knew exactly what her younger sister meant.

"It'll be good to sleep in a bed again," Louise said. "So very good."

"Yes," Beth agreed, lying back on the soft mattress. She closed her eyes. "Mmmm. I don't think I'll ever get up again."

"Not even to see Hank?" Louise couldn't resist the gentle gibe. Since her own plans to draw Hank into her web seemed to have been thwarted, there was no point in begrudging Beth any success she might have with him.

"Oh, Hank's just a boy!" Beth protested, but her cheeks flushed warmly.

"He's only one year younger than you, dear," Louise pointed out. "And he's hardly a boy anymore."

"Well, maybe you're right," Beth mused.

To her own surprise, Louise felt happy that Beth was

interested in Hank. Hank was definitely attracted to her. Louise had seen that on the trail. For a moment, all of her thoughts of revenge and gold and manipulation were gone, and she enjoyed the simple feeling of affection for her sister.

The moment didn't last long, though. There was too much at stake to spend very long wallowing in sentimentality, no matter how good it felt. She had to find Clayborne, had to get her hands on that gold again.

"I believe I'll go downstairs for a few minutes," Louise said. "This room is positively stifling."

"But there's a window you can open."

"No, I need a breath of air and a little walk. You stay here and rest."

Beth frowned. "I suppose that would be all right. . . ."

"Of course it will be. I won't be gone long."

With a smile, Louise shut the room door behind her and turned toward the stairs. She wasn't interested in fresh air. What she really wanted was to work on that desk clerk downstairs, to find out if he had seen any sign of Clayborne or the others in the last few days.

When she reached the lobby, she saw that the clerk wasn't behind the desk. He had probably stepped out for a minute. While she waited she decided that she might as well get that breath of fresh air she had been talking about.

The lobby was empty at the moment, and traffic on the sidewalk had slowed down considerably, she saw as she stepped outside. Down the street, the saloons were still doing a booming business, but this little corner of the town was peaceful at the moment. Louise went to the edge of the hotel porch and leaned on the railing, breathing in the night air. There was a refreshing hint of coolness in it.

"Enjoying yourself, my dear?"

The voice came from close beside her, and she jumped, startled that someone had come up so quietly. And there was something familiar about the voice—

She turned sharply, looked into the insane gray eyes of Thaddeus Kimbell, and started to scream.

Kimbell's left hand shot out and closed around her throat, the hard fingers digging cruelly into her soft flesh. He forced her back, making the porch railing cut painfully into the small of her back.

"Oh, no, we can't have any noise, darling," Kimbell hissed. "Then people would come along and spoil our little reunion, and we don't want that!"

Louise made a soft noise in her throat, but that was all she could manage. She lifted a hand to strike at him, but he warded the blow off easily with his other arm.

"I always knew I would find you," Kimbell said, quickly and quietly. "It was fate that we would be back together. After all, we meant so much to each other, didn't we, Louise? *Didn't we?*" His voice became harsher, more intense, and his grip on her throat tightened. As he repeated the question insistently, she managed to nod her head a fraction of an inch.

"That's right," Kimbell went on. "I loved you, Louise. You know that, don't you? You counted on that. And you and your filthy lover got what you wanted from me. Where's Clayborne?"

Louise couldn't believe that he was able to attack her like this right out in the open. But no one was coming to her aid. The porch was lit by one lamp, but it was over the entrance and the two of them were off to one side. Surely someone would notice and help her, if only he didn't kill her first.

She gestured feebly at her throat, and he eased his grip enough for her to croak, "Don't know . . . where Clayborne is. . . . He left me . . . !"

Kimbell shook his head. "I don't believe that. When I first saw you going into the hotel, I knew Clayborne had to be close by. Now tell me!"

Louise tried futilely to push him away, but he was too strong. As her fingers scrabbled helplessly at him, she suddenly felt a familiar shape at his waist—the hilt of a knife, hanging in a sheath on his belt. Without conscious thought, she plucked it out and thrust it at him.

Kimbell twisted so that the blade passed close by his ribs, then slammed Louise against the railing again. She felt something snap inside when he did that. He kept one hand on her throat while he grabbed her wrist with the other one and savagely bent it back. Again there was a snap of bone and a spasm of pain, and the knife fell.

Kimbell caught it before it could hit the porch. He forced her back farther, bending her almost double over the rail. "Try to kill me, will you?" Both his voice and his body shook with emotion. "I've waited so long. . . ."

He plunged the knife into her body, again and again.

He was barely aware of her screams as his hand slipped off her throat. The flood of crimson over his knife and his hand went almost unnoticed. Instead, he saw the agony in her eyes as he took his revenge.

"Kimbell!"

He ripped the blade from Louise's body at the shout and turned to see Clayborne standing in the hotel doorway. There was a little pistol in his hand, but Kimbell paid no attention to that. His revenge-crazed mind had slipped completely over the edge now. Louise was forgotten, and Clayborne was standing in front of him, ready to die.

"Damn you!" Kimbell howled. "Damn you to hell!" He leaped forward, brandishing the knife.

Clayborne raised the pistol and fired three quick shots. The bullets caught Kimbell in the face, snapping his head back and putting an end to his obsession forever. He fell heavily to his knees, then pitched forward onto his ruined face. The disgrace he had suffered was over.

"Louise?" Clayborne whispered, looking past Kimbell to the bloody form sprawled beside the porch railing.

Her eyes were closed, but she gave a low moan. Clayborne hurried forward and knelt beside her. How in the hell had she come to be here?

"Kimbell's dead, Louise," Clayborne told her. "He

won't bother you again." No one would bother her again, he thought. She didn't have more than a few minutes of life left, not with those wounds.

Her eyelids fluttered open, and she looked up at him with eyes filled with pain and rage. "Abner . . ." she whispered.

"What is it?" he asked, leaning over her. "Can I do something for you?"

"Go . . . to hell . . . you son of a bitch . . . !"

Clayborne couldn't help smiling. So she hadn't changed. No doubt she had followed him here, surviving somehow in the wilderness, driven on by thoughts of revenge. And she had caught up with him just in time to be murdered by that lunatic Kimbell.

"Oh, my God!" Reuben said from behind Clayborne as he took in the scene of carnage on the porch.

"We have to be going," Clayborne said, standing up. "I'm sorry, Louise, but time waits for no man, as I'm sure you know." He looked over his shoulder and spoke sharply to Reed. "Go on down to the stable and make sure the wagons are ready. Espinoza is expecting us at the bridge at ten, and I don't want to be late."

Reed nodded and hurried away, the valise bumping against his leg as he trotted.

Clayborne looked down at Louise again, who was watching him and clutching her bloody middle. "I'm afraid this is good-bye again, dear. This time there won't be any surprises later, though. I'm . . . sorry things didn't work out." He turned on his heel and strode quickly off the porch, hurrying down the street after Reed.

On the porch, Louise closed her eyes. The pain was so bad it had sort of faded away. Her brain couldn't comprehend it. Her head rolled to the side, and she slitted her eyes, opening them just enough that she could see Kimbell lying there, facedown in a pool of blood.

Kimbell, at least, had had some of the revenge he wanted so badly. He had killed her.

* * *

Hank, Enos, and Buffalo stood up and joined the surge of people toward the door of the del Norte. An occasional gunshot was nothing uncommon in El Paso, but there had been three shots this time, close together. An exchange like that usually meant someone had been killed, and that got folks' curiosity up.

It took them a couple of minutes to get through the press of people. When the three of them finally reached the sidewalk, it was just in time to hear someone say, "Came from down at the hotel, I think."

Hank and Buffalo exchanged a quick glance. Louise and Beth were at the hotel. Even as unlikely as it was that they were involved in the shooting, Hank wanted to check it out and be sure. Several people were hurrying up the street toward the hotel, and Hank, Buffalo, and Enos joined them after Buffalo thrust Stink into the hands of the startled bartender for safekeeping.

The desk clerk was on the porch, holding the lamp in his hand now. He was shaking, and the glow from the lamp flickered and swayed. A few people stood in the street in front of the hotel, but none of them seemed to want to go up on the porch.

Two bodies lay there, still and unmoving.

Hank saw them, saw that one of the bodies was that of a woman. His chest began to pound, and he broke into a run. He was barely aware of Enos and Buffalo hurrying along with him. As he drew closer, he saw the woman's dark hair and the familiar gown, once elegant but now tattered and bloody.

"Louise!" Hank heard the cry but didn't know it came from his own throat. He vaulted the porch steps in one leap and pushed aside the clerk, falling to his knees beside the woman. Something was choking him, making it impossible for him to breathe.

Behind him, Enos asked the clerk, "What the hell went on here?"

"I—I don't know," the clerk gulped. "I stepped out

for a cup of coffee, and when I came back I found . . . I heard the shooting. . . ."

Enos turned away from the man in disgust. He wasn't going to find out anything useful there.

Buffalo knelt beside Louise as well, across her body from Hank. "Goddamn," he said in as soft a voice as he could manage. "Poor little lady."

Enos used a booted foot to turn Kimbell's body over. He grimaced when he saw the dead man's face. "Reckon it'll be a chore findin' out who this jasper was," he muttered.

"Beth!" Hank suddenly exclaimed. "We've got to see if Beth's all right!"

He started to get to his feet when he heard the rapid patter of feminine footsteps. Beth came to the door, her face lined with worry, the lamplight reflecting goldenly from her hair. Hank took a quick step and caught her arms.

"Get back inside!" he said urgently. "You don't want to be out here!"

It was too late. Her eyes were riveted on something over his shoulder, and he knew what she was looking at. Her mouth opened wide, but no scream emerged. That would come later.

Enos grabbed the clerk's arm and shoved him forward. "Get the girl inside and keep her there!" Enos ordered. "And send for a doctor!"

Between them, Hank and the clerk were able to get Beth back inside the hotel. The middle-aged woman who did the cooking for the dining room took charge then, taking Beth in tow until the doctor could get there.

That taken care of, Hank, Enos, and Buffalo looked at each other, and Hank put it into words. "What do we do now?"

A low groan from Louise answered the question.

The three men jerked around and bent over her. Given the extent of her wounds, it was a miracle she was still alive. But slowly her eyes opened, and she looked up at them. "Who . . . ?" she asked, in a whisper that could barely be heard.

Hank bent close to her. "Me and Buffalo," he said. "What happened, Louise? Can you tell us?"

"Cl-Clayborne . . ."

Hank's jaw tightened. Inside, he felt like he was about to go flying apart, like a watch wound too tight, but he had to stay in control. He couldn't be a damn crybaby kid. But there had been so much violence, so much death—

It had to end. Tonight.

"Clayborne was here?" he asked.

"He . . . killed Kimbell. . . . Left me here . . . again. Oh, Hank, it . . . Please . . . stop him. . . ."

"Where did he go?"

"Bridge. . . . Meeting a man . . . Espinoza . . . ten o'clock. . . ."

Buffalo asked, "Did he have the gold?"

"Taking . . . wagons across . . . must still be . . . in coffin. . . ."

It was taking every ounce of strength that Louise had left to talk, but she wanted Clayborne stopped more than she wanted to live. She knew she was going to die, Hank thought, and she was telling them her last request.

There was one more, though. Louise tried to lift her head, saying, "Tell Beth . . . I didn't mean . . . I always lov—"

Her head fell back, and the last spark of life flared out in her eyes. After a moment, Hank reached out and gently closed them.

When he knelt the first time beside her body, he had placed the Henry on the floor of the porch. He took it up now, worked the lever to be sure there was a cartridge in the chamber. He stood up.

Enos slipped the Walker Colt out of its holster and took a shell from his belt, slid it into the cylinder under the hammer. "That bridge must be the one down at the

end of Stanton Street," he said. "Espinoza's an undertaker, and he has an office there."

Hank didn't say anything. He stepped off the porch
and began walking toward the bridge.

He still didn't say anything when Enos fell in step to
his right and Buffalo to his left. There was no need for
any talk.

There were still quite a few people standing around in
the street, trying to find out what had happened. They
got out of the way.

Clayborne cursed every second of delay as Ordway
and Smith finished hitching up the teams, assisted by
Jiménez and his sons. He took his watch out again and
glanced at it for what seemed like the dozenth time.
There was still plenty of time, he told himself. If they
weren't there exactly at the stroke of ten, it wouldn't
matter.

He wanted to be across the river before anyone came
looking for him in connection with what had happened
on the hotel porch.

There was something he could do to speed things up
later on, he decided. Reaching into the back of the
Conestoga, he picked up an empty carpetbag he had
selected for this purpose. Turning toward the coffin, he
said to Reed, "Give me a hand, Reuben."

Reed hurried after him. Both men climbed into the
back of the wagon, and Clayborne lifted the lid of the
coffin. "Get that false bottom up," he snapped.

Reed did as he was told, pulling back the lining and
working the catch to free the false bottom. He raised it
with a grunt, revealing the neatly stacked layers of gold.

Clayborne began putting some of the bars into the
carpetbag, much to Reed's surprise. He couldn't keep
himself from bleating, "What's that for?"

"Espinoza will demand payment when we get to the
bridge. I intend to be ready to deliver it to him. Five
thousand dollars was our arrangement, and he had best

not try to raise the price at the last minute." Clayborne closed the bag and hefted it. Heavy, but not too much so. He got down and told Reed, "Close that back up."

He carried the carpetbag to the Conestoga and stowed it on the floorboard of the driver's box. Jiménez, who had seen what was in the coffin, watched him with wide eyes. Clayborne turned to him and said, "You don't mind being paid in gold, do you, amigo?"

Jiménez shook his head vehemently. "No señor, not at all."

Clayborne opened the bag again, reached inside, and took out one bar. "That should cover your trouble and the business you lost by staying closed today at my request. Is that satisfactory?"

"Sí, sí, señor!"

"We're ready," Ordway called. He and Smith went to their horses and swung into the saddle. Each man would be leading part of the little remuda.

"All right," Clayborne said. "Take the reins of your wagon, Reuben." He stepped up onto the Conestoga's box. "Gentlemen, let's move out."

Jiménez's sons opened the doors, and the group went quickly out into the street. Clayborne and Reed turned the wagons toward Stanton Street, Ordway and Smith falling in alongside. As the wagons made the turn onto Stanton, Clayborne whipped his team to more speed, Reed following suit behind. Clayborne peered down the straight stretch of road to the bridge several blocks ahead. Where the devil was Espinoza? Clayborne couldn't spot his carriage anywhere. There was something else up there, though, and his spine suddenly felt icy. Something was wrong.

Standing at the head of the bridge were three men. Waiting.

Twenty

Espinoza was sitting in his carriage near the bridge when he saw the three men walking toward him. One of them was big, with a bushy, scarred face, wearing a filthy blanket poncho and a floppy-brimmed black hat. There was a Sharps rifle in the hands of this one. The second was a tall Texan in dusty range clothes who carried himself with a grace that Espinoza knew well. He had seen it in other men who were very, very good with their guns. The third man was the youngest. He was tall and strong looking, and the Henry rifle he carried seemed to be part of him.

All three of them had the same look in their eyes.

The undertaker hailed them. "You are looking for someone, gentlemen?"

"Abner Clayborne," the youngest one said.

"You have business with him?"

"Damn right," the bearded giant rumbled.

"Then I believe I will take a drive along the river and perhaps return later." Espinoza smiled at them and flicked the reins, starting his team in motion. "Good evening, gentlemen," he said as he drove past them.

"Reckon that was Espinoza," Enos said as they watched the carriage roll away. "Prudent man. I might just look him up later. Got a few things to say to him about his line of work."

"Undertaker, ain't he?" Buffalo asked.

"Like Grandpa," Hank put in. The irony hadn't been lost on him.

Enos shook his head. "Nope," he said to Hank. "Not like your grandpa at all." He hesitated a moment, then went on, "You shouldn't be here, son. You or your friend, either one. This is my job."

"I won't go, Pa. I've got to see the end of it."

Enos couldn't help but smile. "Hell, I know that."

"There they come," Buffalo rumbled.

Standing shoulder to shoulder, they watched the wagons and the riders come down the street toward them. For a moment, Hank thought that Clayborne intended to run them down, and he almost brought the Henry up and started shooting. But when the wagons were less than thirty feet away, Clayborne and Reed hauled up on the reins and brought the teams to a stop.

Clayborne was trying not to stare. He called out, "Young Littleton, isn't it? You've changed, young man."

"Because of you," Hank said coldly.

"I take it you and your companions intend to stop us from crossing into Mexico?"

"That's right." Hank watched Clayborne's face as he went on, "Louise told us you'd be here, before she died."

That news hit Clayborne like a blow, Hank knew. The man had been so convinced he was going to get away. The victory he had so brutally gone after was close now, right across the river.

"Abner Clayborne," Enos said, "you and your men are under arrest for murder and robbery."

"And who might you be?" Clayborne said contemptuously. He glanced over his shoulder, saw Reed sitting tensely on the seat of the other wagon. Reed's right hand was under his jacket, his fingers no doubt wrapped around the butt of his pistol. To either side of the wagon, Ordway and Smith waited, faces calm, hands hovering, ready to draw.

Enos drew a deep breath. "Name's Enos Littleton," he said. "I'm a Texas Ranger."

Reed's nerves broke. He jerked out his gun and fired at Enos, the bullet going high by six feet. He didn't get another chance.

Hank's rifle blurred to his shoulder and blasted in a split second, the slug smacking into Reed's chest and throwing him back off the wagon to tumble into the dusty street.

Ordway and Smith drew and fired, the explosions blending into one. In that same fraction of an instant, Enos went for his gun, and Ordway just had time to realize what a bad mistake they had made.

Enos shot him out of the saddle, spun, and did the same for Smith. They were good, all right; each of them had had time to get a shot off. But both gunmen were dead when they thumped to the street.

Clayborne's little pistol cracked, and Enos felt the slug bite into his shoulder, driving him half around and making the pistol fall from his hand. He hadn't expected that much quickness and accuracy from Clayborne.

The boom of the Sharps filled the street, and Clayborne let out a scream. He looked down at the bloody stump where the slug had blown away his gun and his hand. Buffalo lowered the big rifle as smoke curled from its barrel.

Clayborne's shriek died away, and an awful stillness fell over the street. The sounds of hoofbeats faded into the darkness as the remuda, freed by the deaths of Ordway and Smith, stampeded away. The wagon teams blew and stamped nervously, but they stayed where they were.

"Finish it, younker," Buffalo said.

Hank stared at Clayborne. The man was standing on

the box of the Conestoga, face drained of color. Blood dripped steadily from his arm now that the initial spurting was over. It would be a simple matter to raise the Henry and put a bullet through his brain.

"No," Hank said.

Buffalo stared at him. "That's why you come all this way, ain't it? To kill that bastard?"

"It won't bring my grandpa back, will it?" Hank saw Enos clutching his wounded shoulder and reached out to help support his father. "It's all over."

"The hell it is," Buffalo said. He slipped the Arkansas Toothpick from his belt and strode forward.

"Wait a minute," Enos said. He started to follow, then stopped. He wasn't in any condition to take on Buffalo Newcomb, and he knew it.

Clayborne saw Buffalo coming, and he screamed again. He tried to scramble backward, slipped, and fell to the street. Buffalo reached down with one massive hand and picked him up like he was a baby.

"You've brought a lot of hurt to a lot of folks, mister," Buffalo rumbled. "No more."

He plunged the big knife into Clayborne's belly, ripped it to one side, then the other, then pulled it free and let Clayborne's body fall.

Hank thought about Thomas, about Louise and Ignacio Jiménez and all the others that Abner Clayborne had brought pain and suffering and death to, and still he had to turn away, sickened slightly by what he had just seen.

"I should have stopped him," Enos said.

Hank shook his head. He slipped an arm around Enos's waist and said, "Come on, Pa, let's get you someplace you can sit down."

As he helped Enos over to the sidewalk, moving slowly, Buffalo walked back up the street toward the saloon. Hank wondered where he was going, and a moment later he found out. Buffalo came riding back down the street on his mule, Stink slung in his burlap bag from the saddlehorn, followed by the packhorse. He rode past them, and Hank called out, "Buffalo! What . . . ?"

Buffalo rode to the wagon carrying the coffin and reached out to take the team's harness. Hank's eyes widened.

Buffalo was going to take the gold.

"Hold it, Newcomb!"

Enos's voice rang out, and Hank jerked his head around and saw that his father had gotten up from the sidewalk where he had been sitting. The Colt which Hank had picked up out of the street and slipped back into its holster was in his hand now, and it was rock-steady.

Buffalo rested his hands on the saddlehorn and leaned forward, locking eyes with Enos across the dimly lit street. He waited without saying anything.

"I can't let you take that gold, Newcomb," Enos said. "I should have stopped you from killing Clayborne. Reckon I just thought too much about all the bad things he'd done to my family. But I'll be damned if I'll let you steal that coffin of gold."

Buffalo spat in the dirt. " 'Cause it's your job to take it back where it come from?"

Enos nodded. "That's right."

"You'd shoot me, after all I done for your boy?"

Hank watched Enos's face, saw the play of emotions there. "You just wanted the gold all along," Enos accused.

"Damn right I wanted the gold."

"I won't let you take it."

"Then I reckon you'll just have to plug me, Ranger."

Hank held his breath as Buffalo reined the mule around. He glanced at Enos, saw his finger whitening on the trigger.

And then Enos said, "Hell!" and uncocked the hammer.

Buffalo stopped the mule. He was facing away from them, but Hank could still hear him repeat the heartfelt curse.

Buffalo dropped the lines to the team.

He kneed the mule over next to the Conestoga and reached out, plucked the carpetbag from the floorboard. He ripped it open, glanced inside, grunted in satisfaction. Looking back over his shoulder, he asked, "Reckon they'll ever miss this much?"

Slowly, Enos shook his head.

Hank stepped out into the street. Buffalo grinned at him, the ugly scar on his face making the expression lopsided. "Sorry I never got around to writin' a song 'bout you, boy." Buffalo said. "I'll keep workin' on it, though. Who knows, maybe one day you'll get to hear it after all."

He kicked the mule into a gallop, its hoofbeats echoing hollowly as it thundered across the bridge into Mexico.

Hank watched for a moment as Buffalo Newcomb disappeared into the darkness, then turned and walked back to his father.

Epilogue

It was a simple grave, and the words that Enos said over it were simple as well. But he and Hank and Beth had felt better for having done it.

Beth had been right. She had been able to find the spot where Thomas Littleton's body had been left. Though nothing was left but bones, Hank had dug the grave and they had laid his grandfather's remains to rest. There was no marker, but that didn't matter. Out here a marker wouldn't last long anyway.

The memory of a man, that was what lasted.

Enos's left arm was in a sling, his shoulder still healing from the wound Clayborne had inflicted on him. Though the bullet had been a small caliber, it had done quite a bit of damage. With luck, the doctor in El Paso said, Enos would regain full use of the arm and shoulder. It would take time, though.

Beth's back was healing and the doctor said the scars would fade with time. Just like her emotional scars.

Louise had been buried in El Paso, in a little cemetery with a few cottonwood trees, the mountains looming nearby. Not a bad place at all, Hank thought. Beth had agreed.

They had grown closer in the days following the frenzy of violence and revenge. Beth was alone in the world now, and it seemed the best thing to all of them that she go with Hank and Enos back to San Saba. It was a good town most of the time, a good place to live. Someone there would take her in and make a home for her.

Hank had a feeling that Beth and Dorene Pierson would get along real well. There was a lot that they could give each other. And maybe someday, a few years down the road, if Beth was willing and if he could get up the courage to ask her . . .

"We'd best get moving," Enos said, and Hank was glad his father had interrupted that train of thought. "We can put a few more miles behind us before dark."

They mounted up and rode away from the grave, not looking back. They were in a little valley, and as they came back up onto the plain, they could see the detachment of soldiers that had been sent out to guard the gold on its return trip to Arkansas. The troops had ridden out from a Confederate garrison in east Texas after Enos had sent a dispatch rider to Ranger headquarters with news of the gold's recovery.

Beth had cleared up Kimbell's connection for Enos, and as far as he was concerned, his part of the job was over. He didn't have a thing on his mind now except getting back to San Saba and getting to know his son again. Maybe they could go fishing.

They rejoined the Confederate troop and then rode out in front, taking the point. Hank knew this country now, but he also knew that there was a lot of it still to see. Someday soon, he knew, the wanderlust was going to rise up in him. He'd never be satisfied with having borders on his life again.

"Hank," Beth said as they rode along, "what are you planning to do?"

He glanced sharply at her. Had she read his mind?

There were times when she looked at him that he could swear she knew his every thought. That was another reason he was already starting to think about their future. What was the use of fighting it? And anyway, maybe love wasn't so bad.

"The war won't go on forever," he said, "but Texas will always need Rangers."

"It's a hard life sometimes, son," Enos cautioned.

Hank nodded. "I know. But it's doing something worth doing."

"You're young, Hank. Got a lot of time to think about it yet. But whatever you do, I reckon I'll be proud of you."

Hank smiled, touched by his father's words.

There was something he hadn't told either of them, though, one reason for becoming a Ranger that he hadn't mentioned. One of these years he was going to run across a big, bearded reprobate, and he was going to throw that son of a bitch in jail, possum and all.

Buffalo had promised him a song, by God!

L. J. WASHBURN lives in Azle, Texas, and is the author of *Wild Night* and many published short stories.